Half a Life-Time Ago

And other stories

Elizabeth Cleghorn Gaskell

Half a Life-Time Ago and other stories

Copyright © 2021 Bibliotech Press
All rights reserved

ISBN: 978-1-63637-448-2

CONTENTS

HALF A LIFE-TIME AGO

CHAPTER I

Half a life-time ago, there lived in one of the Westmoreland dales a single woman, of the name of Susan Dixon. She was owner of the small farm-house where she resided, and of some thirty or forty acres of land by which it was surrounded. She had also an hereditary right to a sheep-walk, extending to the wild fells that overhang Blea Tarn. In the language of the country she was a Stateswoman. Her house is yet to be seen on the Oxenfell road, between Skelwith and Coniston. You go along a moorland track, made by the carts that occasionally came for turf from the Oxenfell. A brook babbles and brattles by the wayside, giving you a sense of companionship, which relieves the deep solitude in which this way is usually traversed. Some miles on this side of Coniston there is a farmstead—a gray stone house, and a square of farm-buildings surrounding a green space of rough turf, in the midst of which stands a mighty, funereal umbrageous yew, making a solemn shadow, as of death, in the very heart and centre of the light and heat of the brightest summer day. On the side away from the house, this yard slopes down to a dark-brown pool, which is supplied with fresh water from the overflowings of a stone cistern, into which some rivulet of the brook before-mentioned continually and melodiously falls bubbling. The cattle drink out of this cistern. The household bring their pitchers and fill them with drinking-water by a dilatory, yet pretty, process. The water-carrier brings with her a leaf of the hound's-tongue fern, and, inserting it in the crevice of the gray rock, makes a cool, green spout for the sparkling stream.

The house is no specimen, at the present day, of what it was in the lifetime of Susan Dixon. Then, every small diamond pane in the windows glittered with cleanliness. You might have eaten off the floor; you could see yourself in the pewter plates and the polished oaken awmry, or dresser, of the state kitchen into which you entered. Few strangers penetrated further than this room. Once or twice, wandering tourists, attracted by the lonely picturesqueness of the situation, and the exquisite cleanliness of the house itself, made their way into this house-place, and offered money enough (as they thought) to tempt the hostess to receive them as lodgers. They would give no trouble, they said; they would be out rambling or sketching all day long; would be perfectly content with a share of the food which she provided for herself; or would procure what they required from the Waterhead Inn at Coniston. But no liberal sum—no fair words— moved her from her stony manner, or her monotonous tone of indifferent refusal. No persuasion could induce her to show any more of the house than that first room; no appearance of fatigue procured for the weary an invitation to sit down and rest; and if one more bold and less delicate did so without being asked, Susan stood by, cold and apparently deaf, or only replying by the briefest monosyllables, till the unwelcome visitor had departed. Yet those with whom she had dealings, in the way of selling her cattle or her farm produce, spoke of her as keen after a bargain—a hard one to have to do with; and she never spared herself exertion or fatigue, at market or in the field, to make the most of her produce. She led the hay-makers with her swift, steady rake, and her noiseless evenness of motion. She was about among the earliest in the market, examining samples of oats, pricing them, and then turning with grim satisfaction to her own cleaner corn.

She was served faithfully and long by those who were rather her fellow-labourers than her servants. She was even and just in her dealings with them. If she was peculiar and silent, they knew her, and knew that she might be relied on. Some of them had known her from her childhood; and deep in their hearts was an unspoken—almost unconscious—pity for her, for they knew her story, though they never spoke of it.

Yes; the time had been when that tall, gaunt, hard-featured, angular woman—who never smiled, and hardly ever spoke an unnecessary word—had been a fine-looking girl, bright-spirited and rosy; and when the hearth at the Yew Nook had been as bright as she, with family love and youthful hope and mirth. Fifty or fifty-one years ago, William Dixon and his wife Margaret were alive; and Susan, their daughter, was about eighteen years old—ten years older than the only other child, a boy named after his father. William and Margaret Dixon were rather superior people, of a character belonging—as far as I have seen—exclusively to the class of Westmoreland and Cumberland statesmen—just, independent, upright; not given to much speaking; kind-hearted, but not demonstrative; disliking change, and new ways, and new people; sensible and shrewd; each

3

household self-contained, and its members having little curiosity as to their neighbours, with whom they rarely met for any social intercourse, save at the stated times of sheep-shearing and Christmas; having a certain kind of sober pleasure in amassing money, which occasionally made them miserable (as they call miserly people up in the north) in their old age; reading no light or ephemeral literature, but the grave, solid books brought round by the pedlars (such as the "Paradise Lost" and "Regained,'" "The Death of Abel," "The Spiritual Quixote," and "The Pilgrim's Progress"), were to be found in nearly every house: the men occasionally going off laking, i.e. playing, i.e. drinking for days together, and having to be hunted up by anxious wives, who dared not leave their husbands to the chances of the wild precipitous roads, but walked miles and miles, lantern in hand, in the dead of night, to discover and guide the solemnly-drunken husband home; who had a dreadful headache the next day, and the day after that came forth as grave, and sober, and virtuous looking as if there were no such thing as malt and spirituous liquors in the world; and who were seldom reminded of their misdoings by their wives, to whom such occasional outbreaks were as things of course, when once the immediate anxiety produced by them was over. Such were—such are—the characteristics of a class now passing away from the face of the land, as their compeers, the yeomen, have done before them. Of such was William Dixon. He was a shrewd clever farmer, in his day and generation, when shrewdness was rather shown in the breeding and rearing of sheep and cattle than in the cultivation of land. Owing to this character of his, statesmen from a distance from beyond Kendal, or from Borrowdale, of greater wealth than he, would send their

4

sons to be farm-servants for a year or two with him, in order to learn some of his methods before setting up on land of their own. When Susan, his daughter, was about seventeen, one Michael Hurst was farm-servant at Yew Nook. He worked with the master, and lived with the family, and was in all respects treated as an equal, except in the field. His father was a wealthy statesman at Wythburne, up beyond Grasmere; and through Michael's servitude the families had become acquainted, and the Dixons went over to the High Beck sheep-shearing, and the Hursts came down by Red Bank and Loughrig Tarn and across the Oxenfell when there was the Christmas-tide feasting at Yew Nook. The fathers strolled round the fields together, examined cattle and sheep, and looked knowing over each other's horses. The mothers inspected the dairies and household arrangements, each openly admiring the plans of the other, but secretly preferring their own. Both fathers and mothers cast a glance from time to time at Michael and Susan, who were thinking of nothing less than farm or dairy, but whose unspoken attachment was, in all ways, so suitable and natural a thing that each parent rejoiced over it, although with characteristic reserve it was never spoken about—not even between husband and wife.

Susan had been a strong, independent, healthy girl; a clever help to her mother, and a spirited companion to her father; more of a man in her (as he often said) than her delicate little brother ever would have. He was his mother's darling, although she loved Susan well. There was no positive engagement between Michael and Susan—I doubt whether even plain words of love had been spoken; when one winter-time Margaret Dixon was seized with inflammation consequent upon a neglected cold. She had always been strong and notable, and had been too busy to attend to the early symptoms of illness. It would go off, she said to the woman who helped in the kitchen; or if she did not feel better when they had got the hams and bacon out of hand, she would take some herb-tea and nurse up a bit. But Death could not wait till the hams and bacon were cured: he came on with rapid strides, and shooting arrows of portentous agony. Susan had never seen illness—never knew how much she loved her mother till now, when she felt a dreadful, instinctive certainty that she was losing her. Her mind was thronged with recollections of the many times she had slighted her mother's wishes; her heart was full of the echoes of careless and angry replies that she had spoken. What would she not now give to have opportunities of service and obedience, and trials of her patience and love, for that dear mother who lay gasping in torture! And yet Susan had been a good girl and an affectionate daughter.

The sharp pain went off, and delicious ease came on; yet still her mother sunk. In the midst of this languid peace she was dying. She motioned Susan to her bedside, for she could only whisper; and then, while the father was out of the room, she spoke as much to the eager, hungering eyes of her daughter by the motion of her lips, as by the slow, feeble sounds of her voice.

"Susan, lass, thou must not fret. It is God's will, and thou wilt have a deal to do. Keep father straight if thou canst; and if he goes out Ulverstone ways, see that thou meet him before he gets to the Old Quarry. It's a dree bit for a man who has had a drop. As for lile Will"—Here the poor woman's face began to work and her fingers to move nervously as they lay on the bed-quilt— "lile Will will miss me most of all. Father's often vexed with him because he's not a quick strong lad; he is not, my poor lile chap. And father thinks he's saucy, because he cannot always stomach oat-cake and porridge. There's better than three pound in th' old black tea-pot on the top shelf of the cupboard. Just keep a piece of loaf-bread by you, Susan dear, for Will to come to when he's not taken his breakfast. I have, may be, spoilt him; but there'll be no one to spoil him now."

She began to cry a low, feeble cry, and covered up her face that Susan might not see her. That dear face! those precious moments while yet the eyes could look out with love and intelligence. Susan laid her head down close by her mother's ear.

"Mother I'll take tent of Will. Mother, do you hear? He shall not want ought I can give or get for him, least of all the kind words which you had ever ready for us both. Bless you! bless you! my own mother."

"Thou'lt promise me that, Susan, wilt thou? I can die easy if thou'lt take charge of him. But he's hardly like other folk; he tries father at times, though I think father'll be tender of him when I'm gone, for my sake. And, Susan, there's one thing more. I never spoke on it for fear of the bairn being called a tell-tale, but I just comforted him up. He vexes Michael at times, and Michael has struck him before now. I did not want to make a stir; but he's not strong, and a word from thee, Susan, will go a long way with Michael."

Susan was as red now as she had been pale before; it was the first time that her influence over Michael had been openly acknowledged by a third person, and a flash of joy came athwart

7

the solemn sadness of the moment. Her mother had spoken too much, and now came on the miserable faintness. She never spoke again coherently; but when her children and her husband stood by her bedside, she took lile Will's hand and put it into Susan's, and looked at her with imploring eyes. Susan clasped her arms round Will, and leaned her head upon his little curly one, and vowed within herself to be as a mother to him.

Henceforward she was all in all to her brother. She was a more spirited and amusing companion to him than his mother had been, from her greater activity, and perhaps, also, from her originality of character, which often prompted her to perform her habitual actions in some new and racy manner. She was tender to lile Will when she was prompt and sharp with everybody else—with Michael most of all; for somehow the girl felt that, unprotected by her mother, she must keep up her own dignity, and not allow her lover to see how strong a hold he had upon her heart. He called her hard and cruel, and left her so; and she smiled softly to herself, when his back was turned, to think how little he guessed how deeply he was loved. For Susan was merely comely and fine looking; Michael was strikingly handsome, admired by all the girls for miles round, and quite enough of a country coxcomb to know it and plume himself accordingly. He was the second son of his father; the eldest would have High Beck farm, of course, but there was a good penny in the Kendal bank in store for Michael. When harvest was over, he went to Chapel Langdale to learn to dance; and at night, in his merry moods, he would do his steps on the flag floor of the Yew Nook kitchen, to the secret admiration of Susan, who had never learned dancing, but who flouted him perpetually, even while she admired, in accordance with the rule she seemed to have made for herself about keeping him at a distance so long as he lived under the same roof with her. One evening he sulked at some saucy remark of hers; he sitting in the chimney corner with his arms on his knees, and his head bent forwards, lazily gazing into the wood-fire on the hearth, and luxuriating in rest after a hard day's labour; she sitting among the geraniums on the long, low window-seat, trying to catch the last slanting rays of the autumnal light to enable her to finish stitching a shirt-collar for Will, who lounged full length on the flags at the other side of the hearth to Michael, poking the burning wood from time to time with a long hazel-stick to bring out the leap of glittering sparks.

"And if you can dance a threesome reel, what good does it do ye?" asked Susan, looking askance at Michael, who had just been vaunting his proficiency. "Does it help you plough, reap, or even climb the rocks to take a raven's nest? If I were a man, I'd be ashamed to give in to such softness."

"If you were a man, you'd be glad to do anything which made the pretty girls stand round and admire."

"As they do to you, eh! Ho, Michael, that would not be my way o' being a man!"

"What would then?" asked he, after a pause, during which he had expected in vain that she would go on with her sentence. No answer.

"I should not like you as a man, Susy; you'd be too hard and headstrong."

9

"Am I hard and headstrong?" asked she, with as indifferent a tone as she could assume, but which yet had a touch of pique in it. His quick ear detected the inflexion.

"No, Susy! You're wilful at times, and that's right enough. I don't like a girl without spirit. There's a mighty pretty girl comes to the dancing class; but she is all milk and water. Her eyes never flash like yours when you're put out; why, I can see them flame across the kitchen like a cat's in the dark. Now, if you were a man, I should feel queer before those looks of yours; as it is, I rather like them, because—"

"Because what?" asked she, looking up and perceiving that he had stolen close up to her.

"Because I can make all right in this way," said he, kissing her suddenly.

"Can you?" said she, wrenching herself out of his grasp and panting, half with rage. "Take that, by way of proof that making right is none so easy." And she boxed his ears pretty sharply. He went back to his seat discomfited and out of temper. She could no longer see to look, even if her face had not burnt and her eyes dazzled, but she did not choose to move her seat, so she still preserved her stooping attitude and pretended to go on sewing.

"Eleanor Hebthwaite may be milk-and-water," muttered he, "but—Confound thee, lad! what art thou doing?" exclaimed Michael, as a great piece of burning wood was cast into his face by an unlucky poke of Will's. "Thou great lounging, clumsy chap, I'll teach thee better!" and with one or two good round

10

kicks he sent the lad whimpering away into the back-kitchen. When he had a little recovered himself from his passion, he saw Susan standing before him, her face looking strange and almost ghastly by the reversed position of the shadows, arising from the firelight shining upwards right under it.

"I tell thee what, Michael," said she, "that lad's motherless, but not friendless."

"His own father leathers him, and why should not I, when he's given me such a burn on my face?" said Michael, putting up his hand to his cheek as if in pain.

"His father's his father, and there is nought more to be said. But if he did burn thee, it was by accident, and not o' purpose; as thou kicked him, it's a mercy if his ribs are not broken."

"He howls loud enough, I'm sure. I might ha' kicked many a lad twice as hard, and they'd ne'er ha' said ought but 'damn ye;' but yon lad must needs cry out like a stuck pig if one touches him;" replied Michael, sullenly.

Susan went back to the window-seat, and looked absently out of the window at the drifting clouds for a minute or two, while her eyes filled with tears. Then she got up and made for the outer door which led into the back-kitchen. Before she reached it, however, she heard a low voice, whose music made her thrill, say—

"Susan, Susan!"

Her heart melted within her, but it seemed like treachery to her poor boy, like faithlessness to her dead mother, to turn to her

11

lover while the tears which he had caused to flow were yet unwiped on Will's cheeks. So she seemed to take no heed, but passed into the darkness, and, guided by the sobs, she found her way to where Willie sat crouched among the disused tubs and churns.

"Come out wi' me, lad;" and they went out into the orchard, where the fruit-trees were bare of leaves, but ghastly in their tattered covering of gray moss: and the soughing November wind came with long sweeps over the fells till it rattled among the crackling boughs, underneath which the brother and sister sat in the dark; he in her lap, and she hushing his head against her shoulder.

"Thou should'st na' play wi' fire. It's a naughty trick. Thou'lt suffer for it in worse ways nor this before thou'st done, I'm afeared. I should ha' hit thee twice as lungeous kicks as Mike, if I'd been in his place. He did na' hurt thee, I am sure," she assumed, half as a question.

"Yes but he did. He turned me quite sick." And he let his head fall languidly down on his sister's breast.

"Come, lad! come, lad!" said she anxiously. "Be a man. It was not much that I saw. Why, when first the red cow came she kicked me far harder for offering to milk her before her legs were tied. See thee! here's a peppermint-drop, and I'll make thee a pasty to-night; only don't give way so, for it hurts me sore to think that Michael has done thee any harm, my pretty."

Willie roused himself up, and put back the wet and ruffled hair from his heated face; and he and Susan rose up, and hand-in-

12

hand went towards the house, walking slowly and quietly except for a kind of sob which Willie could not repress. Susan took him to the pump and washed his tear-stained face, till she thought she had obliterated all traces of the recent disturbance, arranging his curls for him, and then she kissed him tenderly, and led him in, hoping to find Michael in the kitchen, and make all straight between them. But the blaze had dropped down into darkness; the wood was a heap of gray ashes in which the sparks ran hither and thither; but even in the groping darkness Susan knew by the sinking at her heart that Michael was not there. She threw another brand on the hearth and lighted the candle, and sat down to her work in silence. Willie cowered on his stool by the side of the fire, eyeing his sister from time to time, and sorry and oppressed, he knew not why, by the sight of her grave, almost stern face. No one came. They two were in the house alone. The old woman who helped Susan with the household work had gone out for the night to some friend's dwelling. William Dixon, the father, was up on the fells seeing after his sheep. Susan had no heart to prepare the evening meal.

"Susy, darling, are you angry with me?" said Willie, in his little piping, gentle voice. He had stolen up to his sister's side. "I won't never play with the fire again; and I'll not cry if Michael does kick me. Only don't look so like dead mother—don't—don't—please don't!" he exclaimed, hiding his face on her shoulder.

"I'm not angry, Willie," said she. "Don't be feared on me. You want your supper, and you shall have it; and don't you be feared on Michael. He shall give reason for every hair of your head that he touches—he shall."

13

When William Dixon came home he found Susan and Willie sitting together, hand-in-hand, and apparently pretty cheerful. He bade them go to bed, for that he would sit up for Michael; and the next morning, when Susan came down, she found that Michael had started an hour before with the cart for lime. It was a long day's work; Susan knew it would be late, perhaps later than on the preceding night, before he returned—at any rate, past her usual bed-time; and on no account would she stop up a minute beyond that hour in the kitchen, whatever she might do in her bed-room. Here she sat and watched till past midnight; and when she saw him coming up the brow with the carts, she knew full well, even in that faint moonlight, that his gait was the gait of a man in liquor. But though she was annoyed and mortified to find in what way he had chosen to forget her, the fact did not disgust or shock her as it would have done many a girl, even at that day, who had not been brought up as Susan had, among a class who considered it no crime, but rather a mark of spirit, in a man to get drunk occasionally. Nevertheless, she chose to hold herself very high all the next day when Michael was, perforce, obliged to give up any attempt to do heavy work, and hung about the out-buildings and farm in a very disconsolate and sickly state. Willie had far more pity on him than Susan. Before evening, Willie and he were fast, and, on his side, ostentatious friends. Willie rode the horses down to water; Willie helped him to chop wood. Susan sat gloomily at her work, hearing an indistinct but cheerful conversation going on in the shippon, while the cows were being milked. She almost felt irritated with her little brother, as if he were a traitor, and had gone over to the enemy in the very battle that she was fighting in his cause. She was alone with no one to speak to, while they prattled on regardless if she were glad or sorry.

14

Soon Willie burst in. "Susan! Susan! come with me; I've something so pretty to show you. Round the corner of the barn—run! run!" (He was dragging her along, half reluctant, half desirous of some change in that weary day.) Round the corner of the barn; and caught hold of by Michael, who stood there awaiting her.

"O Willie!" cried she "you naughty boy. There is nothing pretty—what have you brought me here for? Let me go; I won't be held."

"Only one word. Nay, if you wish it so much, you may go," said Michael, suddenly loosing his hold as she struggled. But now she was free, she only drew off a step or two, murmuring something about Willie.

"You are going, then?" said Michael, with seeming sadness. "You won't hear me say a word of what is in my heart."

"How can I tell whether it is what I should like to hear?" replied she, still drawing back.

"That is just what I want you to tell me; I want you to hear it and then to tell me whether you like it or not."

"Well, you may speak," replied she, turning her back, and beginning to plait the hem of her apron.

He came close to her ear.

"I'm sorry I hurt Willie the other night. He has forgiven me. Can you?"

15

"You hurt him very badly," she replied. "But you are right to be sorry. I forgive you."

"Stop, stop!" said he, laying his hand upon her arm. "There is something more I've got to say. I want you to be my—what is it they call it, Susan?"

"I don't know," said she, half-laughing, but trying to get away with all her might now; and she was a strong girl, but she could not manage it.

"You do. My—what is it I want you to be?"

"I tell you I don't know, and you had best be quiet, and just let me go in, or I shall think you're as bad now as you were last night."

"And how did you know what I was last night? It was past twelve when I came home. Were you watching? Ah, Susan! be my wife, and you shall never have to watch for a drunken husband. If I were your husband, I would come straight home, and count every minute an hour till I saw your bonny face. Now you know what I want you to be. I ask you to be my wife. Will you, my own dear Susan?"

She did not speak for some time. Then she only said "Ask father." And now she was really off like a lapwing round the corner of the barn, and up in her own little room, crying with all her might, before the triumphant smile had left Michael's face where he stood.

The "Ask father" was a mere form to be gone though. Old Daniel Hurst and William Dixon had talked over what they could respectively give their children before this; and that was the parental way of arranging such matters. When the probable amount of worldly gear that he could give his child had been named by each father, the young folk, as they said, might take their own time in coming to the point which the old men, with the prescience of experience, saw they were drifting to; no need to hurry them, for they were both young, and Michael, though active enough, was too thoughtless, old Daniel said, to be trusted with the entire management of a farm. Meanwhile, his father would look about him, and see after all the farms that were to be let.

Michael had a shrewd notion of this preliminary understanding between the fathers, and so felt less daunted than he might otherwise have done at making the application for Susan's hand. It was all right, there was not an obstacle; only a deal of good advice, which the lover thought might have as well been spared, and which it must be confessed he did not much attend to, although he assented to every part of it. Then Susan was called down stairs, and slowly came dropping into view down the steps which led from the two family apartments into the house-place. She tried to look composed and quiet, but it could not be done. She stood side by side with her lover, with her head drooping, her cheeks burning, not daring to look up or move, while her father made the newly-betrothed a somewhat formal address in which he gave his consent, and many a piece of worldly wisdom beside. Susan listened as well as she could for the beating of her heart; but when her father solemnly and sadly referred to his own lost wife, she could keep from sobbing no longer; but throwing her apron over her face, she sat down on

17

the bench by the dresser, and fairly gave way to pent-up tears. Oh, how strangely sweet to be comforted as she was comforted, by tender caress, and many a low-whispered promise of love! Her father sat by the fire, thinking of the days that were gone; Willie was still out of doors; but Susan and Michael felt no one's presence or absence—they only knew they were together as betrothed husband and wife.

In a week, or two, they were formally told of the arrangements to be made in their favour. A small farm in the neighbourhood happened to fall vacant; and Michael's father offered to take it for him, and be responsible for the rent for the first year, while William Dixon was to contribute a certain amount of stock, and both fathers were to help towards the furnishing of the house. Susan received all this information in a quiet, indifferent way; she did not care much for any of these preparations, which were to hurry her through the happy hours; she cared least of all for the money amount of dowry and of substance. It jarred on her to be made the confidante of occasional slight repinings of Michael's, as one by one his future father-in-law set aside a beast or a pig for Susan's portion, which were not always the best animals of their kind upon the farm. But he also complained of his own father's stinginess, which somewhat, though not much, alleviated Susan's dislike to being awakened out of her pure dream of love to the consideration of worldly wealth.

But in the midst of all this bustle, Willie moped and pined. He had the same chord of delicacy running through his mind that made his body feeble and weak. He kept out of the way, and was apparently occupied in whittling and carving uncouth heads on hazel-sticks in an out-house. But he positively avoided

Michael, and shrunk away even from Susan. She was too much occupied to notice this at first. Michael pointed it out to her, saying, with a laugh, —

"Look at Willie! he might be a cast-off lover and jealous of me, he looks so dark and downcast at me." Michael spoke this jest out loud, and Willie burst into tears, and ran out of the house.

"Let me go. Let me go!" said Susan (for her lover's arm was round her waist). "I must go to him if he's fretting. I promised mother I would!" She pulled herself away, and went in search of the boy. She sought in byre and barn, through the orchard, where indeed in this leafless winter-time there was no great concealment; up into the room where the wool was usually stored in the later summer, and at last she found him, sitting at bay, like some hunted creature, up behind the wood-stack.

"What are ye gone for, lad, and me seeking you everywhere?" asked she, breathless.

"I did not know you would seek me. I've been away many a time, and no one has cared to seek me," said he, crying afresh.

"Nonsense," replied Susan, "don't be so foolish, ye little good-for-nought." But she crept up to him in the hole he had made underneath the great, brown sheafs of wood, and squeezed herself down by him. "What for should folk seek after you, when you get away from them whenever you can?" asked she.

"They don't want me to stay. Nobody wants me. If I go with father, he says I hinder more than I help. You used to like to have me with you. But now, you've taken up with Michael, and you'd rather I was away; and I can just bide away; but I cannot

19

stand Michael jeering at me. He's got you to love him and that might serve him."

"But I love you, too, dearly, lad!" said she, putting her arm round his neck.

"Which on us do you like best?" said he, wistfully, after a little pause, putting her arm away, so that he might look in her face, and see if she spoke truth.

She went very red.

"You should not ask such questions. They are not fit for you to ask, nor for me to answer."

"But mother bade you love me!" said he, plaintively.

"And so I do. And so I ever will do. Lover nor husband shall come betwixt thee and me, lad—ne'er a one of them. That I promise thee (as I promised mother before), in the sight of God and with her hearkening now, if ever she can hearken to earthly word again. Only I cannot abide to have thee fretting, just because my heart is large enough for two."

"And thou'lt love me always?"

"Always, and ever. And the more—the more thou'lt love Michael," said she, dropping her voice.

"I'll try," said the boy, sighing, for he remembered many a harsh word and blow of which his sister knew nothing. She would have risen up to go away, but he held her tight, for here and now she was all his own, and he did not know when such a time might come again. So the two sat crouched up and silent, till they heard the horn blowing at the field-gate, which was the summons home to any wanderers belonging to the farm, and at this hour of the evening, signified that supper was ready. Then the two went in.

CHAPTER II

Susan and Michael were to be married in April. He had already gone to take possession of his new farm, three or four miles away from Yew Nook—but that is neighbouring, according to the acceptation of the word in that thinly-populated district,— when William Dixon fell ill. He came home one evening, complaining of head-ache and pains in his limbs, but seemed to loathe the posset which Susan prepared for him; the treacle-posset which was the homely country remedy against an incipient cold. He took to his bed with a sensation of exceeding weariness, and an odd, unusual looking-back to the days of his youth, when he was a lad living with his parents, in this very house.

The next morning he had forgotten all his life since then, and did not know his own children; crying, like a newly-weaned baby, for his mother to come and soothe away his terrible pain. The doctor from Coniston said it was the typhus-fever, and warned Susan of its infectious character, and shook his head over his patient. There were no near friends to come and share her anxiety; only good, kind old Peggy, who was faithfulness itself, and one or two labourers' wives, who would fain have helped her, had not their hands been tied by their responsibility to their own families. But, somehow, Susan neither feared nor flagged. As for fear, indeed, she had no time to give way to it, for every energy of both body and mind was required. Besides, the young have had too little experience of the danger of infection to dread it much. She did indeed wish, from time to time, that Michael had been at home to have taken Willie over to his father's at High Beck; but then, again, the lad was docile and useful to her, and his fecklessness in many things might make him harshly treated by strangers; so, perhaps, it was as well that Michael was away at Appleby fair, or even beyond that—gone into Yorkshire after horses.

Her father grew worse; and the doctor insisted on sending over a nurse from Coniston. Not a professed nurse—Coniston could not have supported such a one; but a widow who was ready to go where the doctor sent her for the sake of the payment. When she came, Susan suddenly gave way; she was felled by the fever herself, and lay unconscious for long weeks. Her consciousness returned to her one spring afternoon; early spring: April,—her wedding-month. There was a little fire burning in the small corner-grate, and the flickering of the blaze was enough for her to notice in her weak state. She felt that there was some one sitting on the window-side of her bed, behind the curtain, but she did not care to know who it was; it was even too great a trouble for her languid mind to consider who it was likely to be. She would rather shut her eyes, and melt off again into the gentle luxury of sleep. The next time she wakened, the Coniston nurse perceived her movement, and made her a cup of tea, which she drank with eager relish; but still they did not speak, and once more Susan lay motionless—not asleep, but strangely, pleasantly conscious of all the small chamber and household sounds; the fall of a cinder on the hearth, the fitful singing of the half-empty kettle, the cattle tramping out to field again after they had been milked, the aged step on the creaking stair—old

Peggy's, as she knew. It came to her door; it stopped; the person outside listened for a moment, and then lifted the wooden latch, and looked in. The watcher by the bedside arose, and went to her. Susan would have been glad to see Peggy's face once more, but was far too weak to turn, so she lay and listened.

"How is she?" whispered one trembling, aged voice.

"Better," replied the other. "She's been awake, and had a cup of tea. She'll do now."

"Has she asked after him?"

"Hush! No; she has not spoken a word."

"Poor lass! poor lass!"

The door was shut. A weak feeling of sorrow and self-pity came over Susan. What was wrong? Whom had she loved? And dawning, dawning, slowly rose the sun of her former life, and all particulars were made distinct to her. She felt that some sorrow was coming to her, and cried over it before she knew what it was, or had strength enough to ask. In the dead of night,—and she had never slept again,—she softly called to the watcher, and asked—

"Who?"

"Who what?" replied the woman, with a conscious affright, ill-veiled by a poor assumption of ease. "Lie still, there's a darling, and go to sleep. Sleep's better for you than all the doctor's stuff."

"Who?" repeated Susan. "Something is wrong. Who?"

"Oh, dear!" said the woman. "There's nothing wrong. Willie has taken the turn, and is doing nicely."

"Father?"

"Well! he's all right now," she answered, looking another way, as if seeking for something.

"Then it's Michael! Oh, me! oh, me!" She set up a succession of weak, plaintive, hysterical cries before the nurse could pacify her, by declaring that Michael had been at the house not three hours before to ask after her, and looked as well and as hearty as ever man did.

"And you heard of no harm to him since?" inquired Susan.

"Bless the lass, no, for sure! I've ne'er heard his name named since I saw him go out of the yard as stout a man as ever trod shoe-leather."

It was well, as the nurse said afterwards to Peggy, that Susan had been so easily pacified by the equivocating answer in respect to her father. If she had pressed the questions home in his case as she did in Michael's, she would have learnt that he was dead and buried more than a month before. It was well, too, that in her weak state of convalescence (which lasted long after this first day of consciousness) her perceptions were not sharp enough to observe the sad change that had taken place in Willie. His bodily strength returned, his appetite was something enormous, but his eyes wandered continually; his regard could not be arrested; his speech became slow, impeded, and incoherent. People began to say that the fever had taken away the little wit Willie Dixon had ever possessed and that they

25

feared that he would end in being a "natural," as they call an idiot in the Dales.

The habitual affection and obedience to Susan lasted longer than any other feeling that the boy had had previous to his illness; and, perhaps, this made her be the last to perceive what every one else had long anticipated. She felt the awakening rude when it did come. It was in this wise:—

One Jane evening, she sat out of doors under the yew-tree, knitting. She was pale still from her recent illness; and her languor, joined to the fact of her black dress, made her look more than usually interesting. She was no longer the buoyant self-sufficient Susan, equal to every occasion. The men were bringing in the cows to be milked, and Michael was about in the yard giving orders and directions with somewhat the air of a master, for the farm belonged of right to Willie, and Susan had succeeded to the guardianship of her brother. Michael and she were to be married as soon as she was strong enough—so, perhaps, his authoritative manner was justified; but the labourers did not like it, although they said little. They remembered a stripling on the farm, knowing far less than they did, and often glad to shelter his ignorance of all agricultural matters behind their superior knowledge. They would have taken orders from Susan with far more willingness; nay, Willie himself might have commanded them; and from the old hereditary feeling toward the owners of land, they would have obeyed him with far greater cordiality than they now showed to Michael. But Susan was tired with even three rounds of knitting, and seemed not to notice, or to care, how things went on around her; and Willie—poor Willie!—there he stood lounging against the door-sill, enormously grown and developed, to be sure, but with restless eyes and ever-open mouth, and every now and then setting up a strange kind of howling cry, and then smiling vacantly to himself at the sound he had made. As the two old labourers passed him, they looked at each other ominously, and shook their heads.

"Willie, darling," said Susan, "don't make that noise—it makes my head ache."

She spoke feebly, and Willie did not seem to hear; at any rate, he continued his howl from time to time.

"Hold thy noise, wilt'a?" said Michael, roughly, as he passed near him, and threatening him with his fist. Susan's back was turned to the pair. The expression of Willie's face changed from vacancy to fear, and he came shambling up to Susan, who put her arm round him, and, as if protected by that shelter, he began making faces at Michael. Susan saw what was going on, and, as if now first struck by the strangeness of her brother's manner, she looked anxiously at Michael for an explanation. Michael was irritated at Willie's defiance of him, and did not mince the matter.

"It's just that the fever has left him silly—he never was as wise as other folk, and now I doubt if he will ever get right."

Susan did not speak, but she went very pale, and her lip quivered. She looked long and wistfully at Willie's face, as he watched the motion of the ducks in the great stable-pool. He laughed softly to himself every now and then.

27

"Willie likes to see the ducks go overhead," said Susan, instinctively adopting the form of speech she would have used to a young child.

"Willie, boo! Willie, boo!" he replied, clapping his hands, and avoiding her eye.

"Speak properly, Willie," said Susan, making a strong effort at self-control, and trying to arrest his attention.

"You know who I am—tell me my name!" She grasped his arm almost painfully tight to make him attend. Now he looked at her, and, for an instant, a gleam of recognition quivered over his face; but the exertion was evidently painful, and he began to cry at the vainness of the effort to recall her name. He hid his face upon her shoulder with the old affectionate trick of manner. She put him gently away, and went into the house into her own little bedroom. She locked the door, and did not reply at all to Michael's calls for her, hardly spoke to old Peggy, who tried to tempt her out to receive some homely sympathy, and through the open easement there still came the idiotic sound of "Willie, boo! Willie, boo!"

28

CHAPTER III

After the stun of the blow came the realization of the consequences. Susan would sit for hours trying patiently to recall and piece together fragments of recollection and consciousness in her brother's mind. She would let him go and pursue some senseless bit of play, and wait until she could catch his eye or his attention again, when she would resume her self-imposed task. Michael complained that she never had a word for him, or a minute of time to spend with him now; but she only said she must try, while there was yet a chance, to bring back her brother's lost wits. As for marriage in this state of uncertainty, she had no heart to think of it. Then Michael stormed, and absented himself for two or three days; but it was of no use. When he came back, he saw that she had been crying till her eyes were all swollen up, and he gathered from Peggy's scoldings (which she did not spare him) that Susan had eaten nothing since he went away. But she was as inflexible as ever.

"Not just yet. Only not just yet. And don't say again that I do not love you," said she, suddenly hiding herself in his arms.

And so matters went on through August. The crop of oats was gathered in; the wheat-field was not ready as yet, when one fine day Michael drove up in a borrowed shandry, and offered to take Willie a ride. His manner, when Susan asked him where he was going to, was rather confused; but the answer was straight and clear enough.

He had business in Ambleside. He would never lose sight of the lad, and have him back safe and sound before dark. So Susan let him go.

Before night they were at home again: Willie in high delight at a little rattling paper windmill that Michael had bought for him in the street, and striving to imitate this new sound with perpetual buzzings. Michael, too, looked pleased. Susan knew the look, although afterwards she remembered that he had tried to veil it from her, and had assumed a grave appearance of sorrow whenever he caught her eye. He put up his horse; for, although he had three miles further to go, the moon was up—the bonny harvest-moon—and he did not care how late he had to drive on such a road by such a light. After the supper which Susan had prepared for the travellers was over, Peggy went up-stairs to see Willie safe in bed; for he had to have the same care taken of him that a little child of four years old requires.

Michael drew near to Susan.

"Susan," said he, "I took Will to see Dr. Preston, at Kendal. He's the first doctor in the county. I thought it were better for us—for you—to know at once what chance there were for him."

"Well!" said Susan, looking eagerly up. She saw the same strange glance of satisfaction, the same instant change to apparent regret and pain. "What did he say?" said she. "Speak! can't you?"

"He said he would never get better of his weakness."

"Never!"

"No; never. It's a long word, and hard to bear. And there's worse to come, dearest. The doctor thinks he will get badder from year to year. And he said, if he was us—you—he would send him off in time to Lancaster Asylum. They've ways there both of keeping such people in order and making them happy. I only tell you what he said," continued he, seeing the gathering storm in her face.

"There was no harm in his saying it," she replied, with great self-constraint, forcing herself to speak coldly instead of angrily. "Folk is welcome to their opinions."

They sat silent for a minute or two, her breast heaving with suppressed feeling.

"He's counted a very clever man," said Michael at length.

"He may be. He's none of my clever men, nor am I going to be guided by him, whatever he may think. And I don't thank them that went and took my poor lad to have such harsh notions formed about him. If I'd been there, I could have called out the sense that is in him."

"Well! I'll not say more to-night, Susan. You're not taking it rightly, and I'd best be gone, and leave you to think it over. I'll not deny they are hard words to hear, but there's sense in them, as I take it; and I reckon you'll have to come to 'em. Anyhow, it's a bad way of thanking me for my pains, and I don't take it well in you, Susan," said he, getting up, as if offended.

"Michael, I'm beside myself with sorrow. Don't blame me if I speak sharp. He and me is the only ones, you see. And mother did so charge me to have a care of him! And this is what he's come to, poor lile chap!" She began to cry, and Michael to comfort her with caresses.

"Don't," said she. "It's no use trying to make me forget poor Willie is a natural. I could hate myself for being happy with you, even for just a little minute. Go away, and leave me to face it out."

"And you'll think it over, Susan, and remember what the doctor says?"

"I can't forget," said she. She meant she could not forget what the doctor had said about the hopelessness of her brother's case; Michael had referred to the plan of sending Willie to an asylum, or madhouse, as they were called in that day and place. The idea had been gathering force in Michael's mind for some time; he had talked it over with his father, and secretly rejoiced over the possession of the farm and land which would then be his in fact, if not in law, by right of his wife. He had always considered the good penny her father could give her in his catalogue of Susan's charms and attractions. But of late he had grown to esteem her as the heiress of Yew Nook. He, too, should have land like his brother—land to possess, to cultivate, to make profit from, to bequeath. For some time he had wondered that Susan had been so much absorbed in Willie's present, that she had never seemed to look forward to his future, state. Michael had long felt the boy to be a trouble; but of late he had absolutely loathed him. His gibbering, his uncouth gestures, his loose, shambling gait, all irritated Michael inexpressibly. He did not come near the Yew Nook for a couple of days. He thought that he would leave her time to become anxious to see him and reconciled to his plan. They were strange lonely days to Susan. They were the first she had spent face to face with the sorrows that had turned her from a girl into a woman; for hitherto Michael had never let twenty-four hours pass by without coming to see her since she had had the fever. Now that he was absent, it seemed as though some cause of irritation was removed from Will, who was much more gentle and tractable than he had been for many weeks. Susan thought that she observed him making efforts at her bidding, and there was something piteous in the way in which he crept up to her, and looked wistfully in her face, as if asking her to restore him the faculties that he felt to be wanting.

"I never will let thee go, lad. Never! There's no knowing where they would take thee to, or what they would do with thee. As it says in the Bible, 'Nought but death shall part thee and me!'"

The country-side was full, in those days, of stories of the brutal treatment offered to the insane; stories that were, in fact, but too well founded, and the truth of one of which only would have been a sufficient reason for the strong prejudice existing against all such places. Each succeeding hour that Susan passed, alone, or with the poor affectionate lad for her sole companion, served to deepen her solemn resolution never to part with him. So, when Michael came, he was annoyed and surprised by the calm way in which she spoke, as if following Dr. Preston's advice was utterly and entirely out of the question. He had expected nothing less than a consent, reluctant it might be, but still a consent; and he was extremely irritated. He could have repressed his anger, but he chose rather to give way to it; thinking that he could thus best work upon Susan's affection, so

33

as to gain his point. But, somehow, he over-reached himself; and now he was astonished in his turn at the passion of indignation that she burst into.

"Thou wilt not bide in the same house with him, say'st thou? There's no need for thy biding, as far as I can tell. There's solemn reason why I should bide with my own flesh and blood and keep to the word I pledged my mother on her death-bed; but, as for thee, there's no tie that I know on to keep thee fro' going to America or Botany Bay this very night, if that were thy inclination. I will have no more of your threats to make me send my bairn away. If thou marry me, thou'lt help me to take charge of Willie. If thou doesn't choose to marry me on those terms— why, I can snap my fingers at thee, never fear. I'm not so far gone in love as that. But I will not have thee, if thou say'st in such a hectoring way that Willie must go out of the house—and the house his own too—before thoul't set foot in it. Willie bides here, and I bide with him."

"Thou hast may-be spoken a word too much," said Michael, pale with rage. "If I am free, as thou say'st, to go to Canada, or Botany Bay, I reckon I'm free to live where I like, and that will not be with a natural who may turn into a madman some day, for aught I know. Choose between him and me, Susy, for I swear to thee, thou shan't have both."

"I have chosen," said Susan, now perfectly composed and still. "Whatever comes of it, I bide with Willie."

"Very well," replied Michael, trying to assume an equal composure of manner. "Then I'll wish you a very good night." He went out of the house door, half-expecting to be called back again; but, instead, he heard a hasty step inside, and a bolt drawn.

"Whew!" said he to himself, "I think I must leave my lady alone for a week or two, and give her time to come to her senses. She'll not find it so easy as she thinks to let me go."

So he went past the kitchen-window in nonchalant style, and was not seen again at Yew Nook for some weeks. How did he pass the time? For the first day or two, he was unusually cross with all things and people that came athwart him. Then wheat-harvest began, and he was busy, and exultant about his heavy crop. Then a man came from a distance to bid for the lease of his farm, which, by his father's advice, had been offered for sale, as he himself was so soon likely to remove to the Yew Nook. He had so little idea that Susan really would remain firm to her determination, that he at once began to haggle with the man who came after his farm, showed him the crop just got in, and managed skilfully enough to make a good bargain for himself. Of course, the bargain had to be sealed at the public-house; and the companions he met with there soon became friends enough to tempt him into Langdale, where again he met with Eleanor Hebthwaite.

How did Susan pass the time? For the first day or so, she was too angry and offended to cry. She went about her household duties in a quick, sharp, jerking, yet absent way; shrinking one moment from Will, overwhelming him with remorseful caresses the next. The third day of Michael's absence, she had the relief of a good fit of crying; and after that, she grew softer and more tender; she felt how harshly she had spoken to him, and

35

remembered how angry she had been. She made excuses for him. "It was no wonder," she said to herself, "that he had been vexed with her; and no wonder he would not give in, when she had never tried to speak gently or to reason with him. She was to blame, and she would tell him so, and tell him once again all that her mother had bade her to be to Willie, and all the horrible stories she had heard about madhouses, and he would be on her side at once."

And so she watched for his coming, intending to apologise as soon as ever she saw him. She hurried over her household work, in order to sit quietly at her sewing, and hear the first distant sound of his well-known step or whistle. But even the sound of her flying needle seemed too loud—perhaps she was losing an exquisite instant of anticipation; so she stopped sewing, and looked longingly out through the geranium leaves, in order that her eye might catch the first stir of the branches in the wood-path by which he generally came. Now and then a bird might spring out of the covert; otherwise the leaves were heavily still in the sultry weather of early autumn. Then she would take up her sewing, and, with a spasm of resolution, she would determine that a certain task should be fulfilled before she would again allow herself the poignant luxury of expectation. Sick at heart was she when the evening closed in, and the chances of that day diminished. Yet she stayed up longer than usual, thinking that if he were coming—if he were only passing along the distant road—the sight of a light in the window might encourage him to make his appearance even at that late hour, while seeing the house all darkened and shut up might quench any such intention.

Very sick and weary at heart, she went to bed; too desolate and despairing to cry, or make any moan. But in the morning hope came afresh. Another day—another chance! And so it went on for weeks. Peggy understood her young mistress's sorrow full well, and respected it by her silence on the subject. Willie seemed happier now that the irritation of Michael's presence was removed; for the poor idiot had a sort of antipathy to Michael, which was a kind of heart's echo to the repugnance in which the latter held him. Altogether, just at this time, Willie was the happiest of the three.

As Susan went into Coniston, to sell her butter, one Saturday, some inconsiderate person told her that she had seen Michael Hurst the night before. I said inconsiderate, but I might rather have said unobservant; for any one who had spent half-an-hour in Susan Dixon's company might have seen that she disliked having any reference made to the subjects nearest her heart, were they joyous or grievous. Now she went a little paler than usual (and she had never recovered her colour since she had had the fever), and tried to keep silence. But an irrepressible pang forced out the question—

"Where?"

"At Thomas Applethwaite's, in Langdale. They had a kind of harvest-home, and he were there among the young folk, and very thick wi' Nelly Hebthwaite, old Thomas's niece. Thou'lt have to look after him a bit, Susan!"

She neither smiled nor sighed. The neighbour who had been speaking to her was struck with the gray stillness of her face. Susan herself felt how well her self-command was obeyed by

37

every little muscle, and said to herself in her Spartan manner, "I can bear it without either wincing or blenching." She went home early, at a tearing, passionate pace, trampling and breaking through all obstacles of briar or bush. Willie was moping in her absence—hanging listlessly on the farm-yard gate to watch for her. When he saw her, he set up one of his strange, inarticulate cries, of which she was now learning the meaning, and came towards her with his loose, galloping run, head and limbs all shaking and wagging with pleasant excitement. Suddenly she turned from him, and burst into tears. She sat down on a stone by the wayside, not a hundred yards from home, and buried her face in her hands, and gave way to a passion of pent-up sorrow; so terrible and full of agony were her low cries, that the idiot stood by her, aghast and silent. All his joy gone for the time, but not, like her joy, turned into ashes. Some thought struck him. Yes! the sight of her woe made him think, great as the exertion was. He ran, and stumbled, and shambled home, buzzing with his lips all the time. She never missed him. He came back in a trice, bringing with him his cherished paper windmill, bought on that fatal day when Michael had taken him into Kendal to have his doom of perpetual idiocy pronounced. He thrust it into Susan's face, her hands, her lap, regardless of the injury his frail plaything thereby received. He leapt before her to think how he had cured all heart-sorrow, buzzing louder than ever. Susan looked up at him, and that glance of her sad eyes sobered him. He began to whimper, he knew not why: and she now, comforter in her turn, tried to soothe him by twirling his windmill. But it was broken; it made no noise; it would not go round. This seemed to afflict Susan more than him. She tried to make it right, although she

38

saw the task was hopeless; and while she did so, the tears rained down unheeded from her bent head on the paper toy.

"It won't do," said she, at last. "It will never do again." And, somehow, she took the accident and her words as omens of the love that was broken, and that she feared could never be pieced together more. She rose up and took Willie's hand, and the two went slowly into the house.

To her surprise, Michael Hurst sat in the house-place. House-place is a sort of better kitchen, where no cookery is done, but which is reserved for state occasions. Michael had gone in there because he was accompanied by his only sister, a woman older than himself, who was well married beyond Keswick, and who now came for the first time to make acquaintance with Susan. Michael had primed his sister with his wishes regarding Will, and the position in which he stood with Susan; and arriving at Yew Nook in the absence of the latter, he had not scrupled to conduct his sister into the guest-room, as he held Mrs. Gale's worldly position in respect and admiration, and therefore wished her to be favourably impressed with all the signs of property which he was beginning to consider as Susan's greatest charms. He had secretly said to himself, that if Eleanor Hebthwaite and Susan Dixon were equal in point of riches, he would sooner have Eleanor by far. He had begun to consider Susan as a termagant; and when he thought of his intercourse with her, recollections of her somewhat warm and hasty temper came far more readily to his mind than any remembrance of her generous, loving nature.

And now she stood face to face with him; her eyes tear-swollen, her garments dusty, and here and there torn in consequence of her rapid progress through the bushy by-paths. She did not make a favourable impression on the well-clad Mrs. Gale, dressed in her best silk gown, and therefore unusually susceptible to the appearance of another. Nor were Susan's manners gracious or cordial. How could they be, when she remembered what had passed between Michael and herself the last time they met? For her penitence had faded away under the daily disappointment of these last weary weeks.

But she was hospitable in substance. She bade Peggy hurry on the kettle, and busied herself among the tea-cups, thankful that the presence of Mrs. Gale, as a stranger, would prevent the immediate recurrence to the one subject which she felt must be present in Michael's mind as well as in her own. But Mrs. Gale was withheld by no such feelings of delicacy. She had come ready-primed with the case, and had undertaken to bring the girl to reason. There was no time to be lost. It had been prearranged between the brother and sister that he was to stroll out into the farm-yard before his sister introduced the subject; but she was so confident in the success of her arguments, that she must needs have the triumph of a victory as soon as possible; and, accordingly, she brought a hail-storm of good reasons to bear upon Susan. Susan did not reply for a long time; she was so indignant at this intermeddling of a stranger in the deep family sorrow and shame. Mrs. Gale thought she was gaining the day, and urged her arguments more pitilessly. Even Michael winced for Susan, and wondered at her silence. He shrank out of sight, and into the shadow, hoping that his sister might prevail, but annoyed at the hard way in which she kept putting the case.

Suddenly Susan turned round from the occupation she had pretended to be engaged in, and said to him in a low voice, which yet not only vibrated itself, but made its hearers thrill through all their obtuseness:

"Michael Hurst! does your sister speak truth, think you?"

Both women looked at him for his answer; Mrs. Gale without anxiety, for had she not said the very words they had spoken together before? had she not used the very arguments that he himself had suggested? Susan, on the contrary, looked to his answer as settling her doom for life; and in the gloom of her eyes you might have read more despair than hope.

He shuffled his position. He shuffled in his words.

"What is it you ask? My sister has said many things."

"I ask you," said Susan, trying to give a crystal clearness both to her expressions and her pronunciation, "if, knowing as you do how Will is afflicted, you will help me to take that charge of him which I promised my mother on her death-bed that I would do; and which means, that I shall keep him always with me, and do all in my power to make his life happy. If you will do this, I will be your wife; if not, I remain unwed."

"But he may get dangerous; he can be but a trouble; his being here is a pain to you, Susan, not a pleasure."

"I ask you for either yes or no," said she, a little contempt at his evading her question mingling with her tone. He perceived it, and it nettled him.

41

"And I have told you. I answered your question the last time I was here. I said I would ne'er keep house with an idiot; no more I will. So now you've gotten your answer."

"I have," said Susan. And she sighed deeply.

"Come, now," said Mrs. Gale, encouraged by the sigh; "one would think you don't love Michael, Susan, to be so stubborn in yielding to what I'm sure would be best for the lad."

"Oh! she does not care for me," said Michael. "I don't believe she ever did."

"Don't I? Haven't I?" asked Susan, her eyes blazing out fire. She left the room directly, and sent Peggy in to make the tea; and catching at Will, who was lounging about in the kitchen, she went up-stairs with him and bolted herself in, straining the boy to her heart, and keeping almost breathless, lest any noise she made might cause him to break out into the howls and sounds which she could not bear that those below should hear.

A knock at the door. It was Peggy.

"He wants for to see you, to wish you good-bye."

"I cannot come. Oh, Peggy, send them away."

It was her only cry for sympathy; and the old servant understood it. She sent them away, somehow; not politely, as I have been given to understand.

"Good go with them," said Peggy, as she grimly watched their retreating figures. "We're rid of bad rubbish, anyhow." And she turned into the house, with the intention of making ready some refreshment for Susan, after her hard day at the market, and her harder evening. But in the kitchen, to which she passed through the empty house-place, making a face of contemptuous dislike at the used tea-cups and fragments of a meal yet standing there, she found Susan, with her sleeves tucked up and her working apron on, busied in preparing to make clap-bread, one of the hardest and hottest domestic tasks of a Daleswoman. She looked up, and first met, and then avoided Peggy's eye; it was too full of sympathy. Her own cheeks were flushed, and her own eyes were dry and burning.

"Where's the board, Peggy? We need clap-bread; and, I reckon, I've time to get through with it to-night." Her voice had a sharp, dry tone in it, and her motions a jerking angularity about them.

Peggy said nothing, but fetched her all that she needed. Susan beat her cakes thin with vehement force. As she stooped over them, regardless even of the task in which she seemed so much occupied, she was surprised by a touch on her mouth of something—what she did not see at first. It was a cup of tea, delicately sweetened and cooled, and held to her lips, when exactly ready, by the faithful old woman. Susan held it off a hand's breath, and looked into Peggy's eyes, while her own filled with the strange relief of tears.

"Lass!" said Peggy, solemnly, "thou hast done well. It is not long to bide, and then the end will come."

"But you are very old, Peggy," said Susan, quivering.

"It is but a day sin' I were young," replied Peggy; but she stopped the conversation by again pushing the cup with gentle

force to Susan's dry and thirsty lips. When she had drunken she
fell again to her labour, Peggy heating the hearth, and doing all
that she knew would be required, but never speaking another
word. Willie basked close to the fire, enjoying the animal luxury
of warmth, for the autumn evenings were beginning to be chilly.
It was one o'clock before they thought of going to bed on that
memorable night.

CHAPTER IV

The vehemence with which Susan Dixon threw herself into occupation could not last for ever. Times of languor and remembrance would come—times when she recurred with a passionate yearning to bygone days, the recollection of which was so vivid and delicious, that it seemed as though it were the reality, and the present bleak bareness the dream. She smiled anew at the magical sweetness of some touch or tone which in memory she felt and heard, and drank the delicious cup of poison, although at the very time she knew what the consequences of racking pain would be.

"This time, last year," thought she, "we went nutting together— this very day last year; just such a day as to-day. Purple and gold were the lights on the hills; the leaves were just turning brown; here and there on the sunny slopes the stubble-fields looked tawny; down in a cleft of yon purple slate-rock the beck fell like a silver glancing thread; all just as it is to-day. And he climbed the slender, swaying nut-trees, and bent the branches for me to gather; or made a passage through the hazel copses, from time to time claiming a toll. Who could have thought he loved me so little?—who?—who?"

Or, as the evening closed in, she would allow herself to imagine that she heard his coming step, just that she might recall time feeling of exquisite delight which had passed by without the due and passionate relish at the time. Then she would wonder how

45

she could have had strength, the cruel, self-piercing strength, to say what she had done; to stab himself with that stern resolution, of which the sear would remain till her dying day. It might have been right; but, as she sickened, she wished she had not instinctively chosen the right. How luxurious a life haunted by no stern sense of duty must be! And many led this kind of life; why could not she? O, for one hour again of his sweet company! If he came now, she would agree to whatever he proposed.

It was a fever of the mind. She passed through it, and came out healthy, if weak. She was capable once more of taking pleasure in following an unseen guide through briar and brake. She returned with tenfold affection to her protecting care of Willie. She acknowledged to herself that he was to be her all-in-all in life. She made him her constant companion. For his sake, as the real owner of Yew Nook, and she as his steward and guardian, she began that course of careful saving, and that love of acquisition, which afterwards gained for her the reputation of being miserly. She still thought that he might regain a scanty portion of sense—enough to require some simple pleasures and excitement, which would cost money. And money should not be wanting. Peggy rather assisted her in the formation of her parsimonious habits than otherwise; economy was the order of the district, and a certain degree of respectable avarice the characteristic of her age. Only Willie was never stinted nor hindered of anything that the two women thought could give him pleasure, for want of money.

There was one gratification which Susan felt was needed for the restoration of her mind to its more healthy state, after she had passed through the whirling fever, when duty was as nothing, and anarchy reigned; a gratification that, somehow, was to be her last burst of unreasonableness; of which she knew and recognised pain as the sure consequence. She must see him once more,—herself unseen.

The week before the Christmas of this memorable year, she went out in the dusk of the early winter evening, wrapped close in shawl and cloak. She wore her dark shawl under her cloak, putting it over her head in lieu of a bonnet; for she knew that she might have to wait long in concealment. Then she tramped over the wet fell-path, shut in by misty rain for miles and miles, till she came to the place where he was lodging; a farm-house in Langdale, with a steep, stony lane leading up to it: this lane was entered by a gate out of the main road, and by the gate were a few bushes—thorns; but of them the leaves had fallen, and they offered no concealment: an old wreck of a yew-tree grew among them, however, and underneath that Susan cowered down, shrouding her face, of which the colour might betray her, with a corner of her shawl. Long did she wait; cold and cramped she became, too damp and stiff to change her posture readily. And after all, he might never come! But, she would wait till daylight, if need were; and she pulled out a crust, with which she had providently supplied herself. The rain had ceased,—a dull, still, brooding weather had succeeded; it was a night to hear distant sounds. She heard horses' hoofs striking and splashing in the stones, and in the pools of the road at her back. Two horses; not well-ridden, or evenly guided, as she could tell.

Michael Hurst and a companion drew near: not tipsy, but not sober. They stopped at the gate to bid each other a maudlin farewell. Michael stooped forward to catch the latch with the hook of the stick which he carried; he dropped the stick, and it fell with one end close to Susan,—indeed, with the slightest change of posture she could have opened the gate for him. He swore a great oath, and struck his horse with his closed fist, as if that animal had been to blame; then he dismounted, opened the gate, and fumbled about for his stick. When he had found it (Susan had touched the other end) his first use of it was to flog his horse well, and she had much ado to avoid its kicks and plunges. Then, still swearing, he staggered up the lane, for it was evident he was not sober enough to remount.

By daylight Susan was back and at her daily labours at Yew Nook. When the spring came, Michael Hurst was married to Eleanor Hebthwaite. Others, too, were married, and christenings made their firesides merry and glad; or they travelled, and came back after long years with many wondrous tales. More rarely, perhaps, a Dalesman changed his dwelling. But to all households more change came than to Yew Nook. There the seasons came round with monotonous sameness; or, if they brought mutation, it was of a slow, and decaying, and depressing kind. Old Peggy died. Her silent sympathy, concealed under much roughness, was a loss to Susan Dixon. Susan was not yet thirty when this happened, but she looked a middle-aged, not to say an elderly woman. People affirmed that she had never recovered her complexion since that fever, a dozen years ago, which killed her father, and left Will Dixon an idiot. But besides her gray sallowness, the lines in her face were strong, and deep, and hard. The movements of her eyeballs were slow and heavy; the wrinkles at the corners of her mouth and eyes were planted firm and sure; not an ounce of

48

unnecessary flesh was there on her bones—every muscle started strong and ready for use. She needed all this bodily strength, to a degree that no human creature, now Peggy was dead, knew of: for Willie had grown up large and strong in body, and, in general, docile enough in mind; but, every now and then, he became first moody, and then violent. These paroxysms lasted but a day or two; and it was Susan's anxious care to keep their very existence hidden and unknown. It is true, that occasional passers-by on that lonely road heard sounds at night of knocking about of furniture, blows, and cries, as of some tearing demon within the solitary farm-house; but these fits of violence usually occurred in the night; and whatever had been their consequence, Susan had tidied and redded up all signs of aught unusual before the morning. For, above all, she dreaded lest some one might find out in what danger and peril she occasionally was, and might assume a right to take away her brother from her care. The one idea of taking charge of him had deepened and deepened with years. It was graven into her mind as the object for which she lived. The sacrifice she had made for this object only made it more precious to her. Besides, she separated the idea of the docile, affectionate, loutish, indolent Will, and kept it distinct from the terror which the demon that occasionally possessed him inspired her with. The one was her flesh and her blood—the child of her dead mother; the other was some fiend who came to torture and convulse the creature she so loved. She believed that she fought her brother's battle in holding down those tearing hands, in binding whenever she could those uplifted restless arms prompt and prone to do mischief. All the time she subdued him with her cunning or her strength, she spoke to him in pitying murmurs, or abused the third person,

49

the fiendish enemy, in no unmeasured tones. Towards morning the paroxysm was exhausted, and he would fall asleep, perhaps only to waken with evil and renewed vigour. But when he was laid down, she would sally out to taste the fresh air, and to work off her wild sorrow in cries and mutterings to herself. The early labourers saw her gestures at a distance, and thought her as crazed as the idiot-brother who made the neighbourhood a haunted place. But did any chance person call at Yew Nook later on in the day, he would find Susan Dixon cold, calm, collected; her manner curt, her wits keen.

Once this fit of violence lasted longer than usual. Susan's strength both of mind and body was nearly worn out; she wrestled in prayer that somehow it might end before she, too, was driven mad; or, worse, might be obliged to give up life's aim, and consign Willie to a madhouse. From that moment of prayer (as she afterwards superstitiously thought) Willie calmed—and then he drooped—and then he sank—and, last of all, he died in reality from physical exhaustion.

But he was so gentle and tender as he lay on his dying bed; such strange, child-like gleams of returning intelligence came over his face, long after the power to make his dull, inarticulate sounds had departed, that Susan was attracted to him by a stronger tie than she had ever felt before. It was something to have even an idiot loving her with dumb, wistful, animal affection; something to have any creature looking at her with such beseeching eyes, imploring protection from the insidious enemy stealing on. And yet she knew that to him death was no enemy, but a true friend, restoring light and health to his poor clouded mind. It was to her that death was an enemy; to her, the survivor, when Willie died; there was no one to love her.

Worse doom still, there was no one left on earth for her to love.

You now know why no wandering tourist could persuade her to receive him as a lodger; why no tired traveller could melt her heart to afford him rest and refreshment; why long habits of seclusion had given her a moroseness of manner, and how care for the interests of another had rendered her keen and miserly.

But there was a third act in the drama of her life.

CHAPTER V

In spite of Peggy's prophecy that Susan's life should not seem long, it did seem wearisome and endless, as the years slowly uncoiled their monotonous circles. To be sure, she might have made change for herself, but she did not care to do it. It was, indeed, more than "not caring," which merely implies a certain degree of vis inertiæ to be subdued before an object can be attained, and that the object itself does not seem to be of sufficient importance to call out the requisite energy. On the contrary, Susan exerted herself to avoid change and variety. She had a morbid dread of new faces, which originated in her desire to keep poor dead Willie's state a profound secret. She had a contempt for new customs; and, indeed, her old ways prospered so well under her active hand and vigilant eye, that it was difficult to know how they could be improved upon. She was regularly present in Coniston market with the best butter and the earliest chickens of the season. Those were the common farm produce that every farmer's wife about had to sell; but Susan, after she had disposed of the more feminine articles, turned to on the man's side. A better judge of a horse or cow there was not in all the country round. Yorkshire itself might have attempted to jockey her, and would have failed. Her corn was sound and clean; her potatoes well preserved to the latest spring. People began to talk of the hoards of money Susan Dixon must have laid up somewhere; and one young ne'er-do-weel of a farmer's son undertook to make love to the woman of forty, who looked fifty-five, if a day. He made up to her by opening a gate on the road-path home, as she was riding on a bare-backed horse, her purchase not an hour ago. She was off before him, refusing his civility; but the remounting was not so easy, and rather than fail she did not choose to attempt it. She walked, and he walked alongside, improving his opportunity, which, as he vainly thought, had been consciously granted to him. As they drew near Yew Nook, he ventured on some expression of a wish to keep company with her. His words were vague and clumsily arranged. Susan turned round and coolly asked him to explain himself, he took courage, as he thought of her reputed wealth, and expressed his wishes this second time pretty plainly. To his surprise, the reply she made was in a series of smart strokes across his shoulders, administered through the medium of a supple hazel-switch.

"Take that!" said she, almost breathless, "to teach thee how thou darest make a fool of an honest woman old enough to be thy mother. If thou com'st a step nearer the house, there's a good horse-pool, and there's two stout fellows who'll like no better fun than ducking thee. Be off wi' thee!"

And she strode into her own premises, never looking round to see whether he obeyed her injunction or not.

Sometimes three or four years would pass over without her hearing Michael Hurst's name mentioned. She used to wonder at such times whether he were dead or alive. She would sit for hours by the dying embers of her fire on a winter's evening, trying to recall the scenes of her youth; trying to bring up living pictures of the faces she had then known—Michael's most

53

especially. She thought it was possible, so long had been the lapse of years, that she might now pass by him in the street unknowing and unknown. His outward form she might not recognize, but himself she should feel in the thrill of her whole being. He could not pass her unawares.

What little she did hear about him, all testified a downward tendency. He drank—not at stated times when there was no other work to be done, but continually, whether it was seed-time or harvest. His children were all ill at the same time; then one died, while the others recovered, but were poor sickly things. No one dared to give Susan any direct intelligence of her former lover; many avoided all mention of his name in her presence; but a few spoke out either in indifference to, or ignorance of, those bygone days. Susan heard every word, every whisper, every sound that related to him. But her eye never changed, nor did a muscle of her face move.

Late one November night she sat over her fire; not a human being besides herself in the house; none but she had ever slept there since Willie's death. The farm-labourers had foddered the cattle and gone home hours before. There were crickets chirping all round the warm hearth-stones; there was the clock ticking with the peculiar beat Susan had known from her childhood, and which then and ever since she had oddly associated within the idea of a mother and child talking together, one loud tick, and quick—a feeble, sharp one following.

The day had been keen, and piercingly cold. The whole lift of heaven seemed a dome of iron. Black and frost-bound was the earth under the cruel east wind. Now the wind had dropped, and as the darkness had gathered in, the weather-wise old labourers prophesied snow. The sounds in the air arose again, as Susan sat still and silent. They were of a different character to what they had been during the prevalence of the east wind. Then they had been shrill and piping; now they were like low distant growling; not unmusical, but strangely threatening. Susan went to the window, and drew aside the little curtain. The whole world was white—the air was blinded with the swift and heavy fall of snow. At present it came down straight, but Susan knew those distant sounds in the hollows and gulleys of the hills portended a driving wind and a more cruel storm. She thought of her sheep; were they all folded? the new-born calf, was it bedded well? Before the drifts were formed too deep for her to pass in and out—and by the morning she judged that they would be six or seven feet deep—she would go out and see after the comfort of her beasts. She took a lantern, and tied a shawl over her head, and went out into the open air. She had tenderly provided for all her animals, and was returning, when, borne on the blast as if some spirit-cry—for it seemed to come rather down from the skies than from any creature standing on earth's level—she heard a voice of agony; she could not distinguish words; it seemed rather as if some bird of prey was being caught in the whirl of the icy wind, and torn and tortured by its violence. Again up high above! Susan put down her lantern, and shouted loud in return; it was an instinct, for if the creature were not human, which she had doubted but a moment before, what good could her responding cry do? And her cry was seized on by the tyrannous wind, and borne farther away in the opposite direction to that from which the call of agony had proceeded. Again she listened; no sound: then again it rang through space; and this time she was sure it was human. She turned into the house, and heaped turf and wood on the fire, which, careless of her own sensations, she had allowed to fade and almost die out. She put a new candle in her lantern; she changed her shawl for a maud, and leaving the door on latch, she sallied out. Just at the moment when her ear first encountered the weird noises of the storm, on issuing forth into the open air, she thought she heard the words, "O God! O help!" They were a guide to her, if words they were, for they came straight from a rock not a quarter of a mile from Yew Nook, but only to be reached, on account of its precipitous character, by a round-about path. Thither she steered, defying wind and snow; guided by here a thorn-tree, there an old, doddered oak, which had not quite lest their identity under the whelming mask of snow. Now and then she stopped to listen; but never a word or sound heard she, till right from where the copse-wood grew thick and tangled at the base of the rock, round which she was winding, she heard a moan. Into the brake—all snow in appearance—almost a plain of snow looked on from the little eminence where she stood—she plunged, breaking down the bush, stumbling, bruising herself, fighting her way; her lantern held between her teeth, and she herself using head as well as hands to butt away a passage, at whatever cost of bodily injury. As she climbed or staggered, owing to the unevenness of the snow-covered ground, where the briars and weeds of years were tangled and matted together, her foot felt something strangely soft and yielding. She lowered her lantern; there lay a man, prone on his face, nearly covered by the fast-falling flakes; he must have fallen from the rock above, as, not knowing of the circuitous path, he had tried to descend its steep, slippery face.

56

Who could tell? it was no time for thinking. Susan lifted him up with her wiry strength; he gave no help—no sign of life; but for all that he might be alive: he was still warm; she tied her maud round him; she fastened the lantern to her apron-string; she held him tight: half-carrying, half-dragging—what did a few bruises signify to him, compared to dear life, to precious life! She got him through the brake, and down the path. There, for an instant, she stopped to take breath; but, as if stung by the Furies, she pushed on again with almost superhuman strength. Clasping him round the waist, and leaning his dead weight against the lintel of the door, she tried to undo the latch; but now, just at this moment, a trembling faintness came over her, and a fearful dread took possession of her—that here, on the very threshold of her home, she might be found dead, and buried under the snow, when the farm-servants came in the morning. This terror stirred her up to one more effort. Then she and her companion were in the warmth of the quiet haven of that kitchen; she laid him on the settle, and sank on the floor by his side. How long she remained in this swoon she could not tell; not very long she judged by the fire, which was still red and sullenly glowing when she came to herself. She lighted the candle, and bent over her late burden to ascertain if indeed he were dead. She stood long gazing. The man lay dead. There could be no doubt about it. His filmy eyes glared at her, unshut. But Susan was not one to be affrighted by the stony aspect of death. It was not that; it was the bitter, woeful recognition of Michael Hurst!

She was convinced he was dead; but after a while she refused to believe in her conviction. She stripped off his wet outer-garments with trembling, hurried hands. She brought a blanket down from her own bed; she made up the fire. She swathed him in fresh, warm wrappings, and laid him on the flags before the fire, sitting herself at his head, and holding it in her lap, while she tenderly wiped his loose, wet hair, curly still, although its colour had changed from nut-brown to iron-gray since she had seen it last. From time to time she bent over the face afresh, sick, and fain to believe that the flicker of the fire-light was some slight convulsive motion. But the dim, staring eyes struck chill to her heart. At last she ceased her delicate, busy cares: but she still held the head softly, as if caressing it. She thought over all the possibilities and chances in the mingled yarn of their lives that might, by so slight a turn, have ended far otherwise. If her mother's cold had been early tended, so that the responsibility as to her brother's weal or woe had not fallen upon her; if the fever had not taken such rough, cruel hold on Will; nay, if Mrs. Gale, that hard, worldly sister, had not accompanied him on his last visit to Yew Nook—his very last before this fatal, stormy might; if she had heard his cry,—cry uttered by these pale, dead lips with such wild, despairing agony, not yet three hours ago!—O! if she had but heard it sooner, he might have been saved before that blind, false step had precipitated him down the rock! In going over this weary chain of unrealized possibilities, Susan learnt the force of Peggy's words. Life was short, looking back upon it. It seemed but yesterday since all the love of her being had been poured out, and run to waste. The intervening years— the long monotonous years that had turned her into an old woman before her time—were but a dream.

The labourers coming in the dawn of the winter's day were

surprised to see the fire-light through the low kitchen-window. They knocked, and hearing a moaning answer, they entered, fearing that something had befallen their mistress. For all explanation they got these words

"It is Michael Hurst. He was belated, and fell down the Raven's Crag. Where does Eleanor, his wife, live?"

How Michael Hurst got to Yew Nook no one but Susan ever knew. They thought he had dragged himself there, with some sore internal bruise sapping away his minuted life. They could not have believed the superhuman exertion which had first sought him out, and then dragged him hither. Only Susan knew of that.

She gave him into the charge of her servants, and went out and saddled her horse. Where the wind had drifted the snow on one side, and the road was clear and bare, she rode, and rode fast; where the soft, deceitful heaps were massed up, she dismounted and led her steed, plunging in deep, with fierce energy, the pain at her heart urging her onwards with a sharp, digging spur.

The gray, solemn, winter's noon was more night-like than the depth of summer's night; dim-purple brooded the low skies over the white earth, as Susan rode up to what had been Michael Hurst's abode while living. It was a small farm-house carelessly kept outside, slatternly tended within. The pretty Nelly Hebthwaite was pretty still; her delicate face had never suffered from any long-enduring feeling. If anything, its expression was that of plaintive sorrow; but the soft, light hair had scarcely a tinge of gray; the wood-rose tint of complexion yet remained, if not so brilliant as in youth; the straight nose, the small mouth were untouched by time. Susan felt the contrast even at that moment. She knew that her own skin was weather-beaten, furrowed, brown,—that her teeth were gone, and her hair gray and ragged. And yet she was not two years older than Nelly,— she had not been, in youth, when she took account of these things. Nelly stood wondering at the strange-enough horse-woman, who stopped and panted at the door, holding her horse's bridle, and refusing to enter.

"Where is Michael Hurst?" asked Susan, at last.

"Well, I can't rightly say. He should have been at home last night, but he was off, seeing after a public-house to be let at Ulverstone, for our farm does not answer, and we were thinking—"

"He did not come home last night?" said Susan, cutting short the story, and half-affirming, half-questioning, by way of letting in a ray of the awful light before she let it full in, in its consuming wrath.

"No! he'll be stopping somewhere out Ulverstone ways. I'm sure we've need of him at home, for I've no one but lile Tommy to help me tend the beasts. Things have not gone well with us, and we don't keep a servant now. But you're trembling all over, ma'am. You'd better come in, and take something warm, while your horse rests. That's the stable-door, to your left."

Susan took her horse there; loosened his girths, and rubbed him down with a wisp of straw. Then she hooked about her for hay; but the place was bare of feed, and smelt damp and unused. She went to the house, thankful for the respite, and got some clap-bread, which she mashed up in a pailful of lukewarm water. Every moment was a respite, and yet every moment made her dread the more the task that lay before her. It would be longer than she thought at first. She took the saddle off, and hung about her horse, which seemed, somehow, more like a friend than anything else in the world. She laid her cheek against its neck, and rested there, before returning to the house for the last time.

Eleanor had brought down one of her own gowns, which hung on a chair against the fire, and had made her unknown visitor a cup of hot tea. Susan could hardly bear all these little attentions: they choked her, and yet she was so wet, so weak with fatigue and excitement, that she could neither resist by voice or by action. Two children stood awkwardly about, puzzled at the scene, and even Eleanor began to wish for some explanation of who her strange visitor was.

"You've, maybe, heard him speaking of me? I'm called Susan Dixon."
Nelly coloured, and avoided meeting Susan's eye.

"I've heard other folk speak of you. He never named your name."

This respect of silence came like balm to Susan: balm not felt or heeded at the time it was applied, but very grateful in its effects for all that.

"He is at my house," continued Susan, determined not to stop or quaver in the operation—the pain which must be inflicted.

"At your house? Yew Nook?" questioned Eleanor, surprised. "How came he there?"—half jealously. "Did he take shelter from the coming storm? Tell me,—there is something—tell me, woman!"

"He took no shelter. Would to God he had!"

"O! would to God! would to God!" shrieked out Eleanor, learning all from the woful import of those dreary eyes. Her cries thrilled through the house; the children's piping wailings and passionate cries on "Daddy! Daddy!" pierced into Susan's very marrow. But she remained as still and tearless as the great round face upon the clock.

At last, in a lull of crying, she said,—not exactly questioning, but as if partly to herself—

"You loved him, then?"

"Loved him! he was my husband! He was the father of three bonny bairns that lie dead in Grasmere churchyard. I wish you'd go, Susan Dixon, and let me weep without your watching me! I wish you'd never come near the place."

"Alas! alas! it would not have brought him to life. I would have laid down my own to save his. My life has been so very sad! No one would have cared if I had died. Alas! alas!"

The tone in which she said this was so utterly mournful and despairing that it awed Nelly into quiet for a time. But by-and-by she said, "I would not turn a dog out to do it harm; but the night is clear, and Tommy shall guide you to the Red Cow. But, oh, I want to be alone! If you'll come back to-morrow, I'll be better, and I'll hear all, and thank you for every kindness you have shown him,—and I do believe you've showed him kindness,—though I don't know why."

Susan moved heavily and strangely.

She said something—her words came thick and unintelligible. She had had a paralytic stroke since she had last spoken. She could not go, even if she would. Nor did Eleanor, when she became aware of the state of the case, wish her to leave. She had her laid on her own bed, and weeping silently all the while for her lost husband, she nursed Susan like a sister. She did not know what her guest's worldly position might be; and she might never be repaid. But she sold many a little trifle to purchase such small comforts as Susan needed. Susan, lying still and motionless, learnt much. It was not a severe stroke; it might be the forerunner of others yet to come, but at some distance of time. But for the present she recovered, and regained much of her former health. On her sick-bed she matured her plans. When she returned to Yew Nook, she took Michael Hurst's widow and children with her to live there, and fill up the haunted hearth with living forms that should banish the ghosts.

And so it fell out that the latter days of Susan Dixon's life were better than the former.

AN ACCURSED RACE

We have our prejudices in England. Or, if that assertion offends any of my readers, I will modify it: we have had our prejudices in England. We have tortured Jews; we have burnt Catholics and Protestants, to say nothing of a few witches and wizards. We have satirized Puritans, and we have dressed-up Guys. But, after all, I do not think we have been so bad as our Continental friends. To be sure, our insular position has kept us free, to a certain degree, from the inroads of alien races; who, driven from one land of refuge, steal into another equally unwilling to receive them; and where, for long centuries, their presence is barely endured, and no pains is taken to conceal the repugnance which the natives of "pure blood" experience towards them.

There yet remains a remnant of the miserable people called Cagots in the valleys of the Pyrenees; in the Landes near Bourdeaux; and, stretching up on the west side of France, their numbers become larger in Lower Brittany. Even now, the origin of these families is a word of shame to them among their neighbours; although they are protected by the law, which confirmed them in the equal rights of citizens about the end of the last century. Before then they had lived, for hundreds of years, isolated from all those who boasted of pure blood, and they had been, all this time, oppressed by cruel local edicts. They were truly what they were popularly called, The Accursed Race.

All distinct traces of their origin are lost. Even at the close of that period which we call the Middle Ages, this was a problem which no one could solve; and as the traces, which even then were faint and uncertain, have vanished away one by one, it is a complete mystery at the present day. Why they were accursed in the first instance, why isolated from their kind, no one knows. From the earliest accounts of their state that are yet remaining to us, it seems that the names which they gave each other were ignored by the population they lived amongst, who spoke of them as Crestiaa, or Cagots, just as we speak of animals by their generic names. Their houses or huts were always placed at some distance out of the villages of the country-folk, who unwillingly called in the services of the Cagots as carpenters, or tilers, or slaters—trades which seemed appropriated by this unfortunate race—who were forbidden to occupy land, or to bear arms, the usual occupations of those times. They had some small right of pasturage on the common lands, and in the forests: but the number of their cattle and live-stock was strictly limited by the earliest laws relating to the Cagots. They were forbidden by one act to have more than twenty sheep, a pig, a ram, and six geese. The pig was to be fattened and killed for winter food; the fleece of the sheep was to clothe them; but if the said sheep had lambs, they were forbidden to eat them. Their only privilege arising from this increase was, that they might choose out the strongest and finest in preference to keeping the old sheep. At Martinmas the authorities of the commune came round, and counted over the stock of each Cagot. If he had more than his appointed number, they were forfeited; half went to the commune, half to the baillie, or chief magistrate of the commune. The poor beasts were limited as to the amount of common which they might stray over in search of grass. While the cattle of the inhabitants of the commune might wander hither and thither in search of the sweetest herbage, the deepest shade, or the coolest pool in which to stand on the hot days, and lazily switch their dappled sides, the Cagot sheep and pig had to learn imaginary bounds, beyond which if they strayed, any one might snap them up, and kill them, reserving a part of the flesh for his own use, but graciously restoring the inferior parts to their original owner. Any damage done by the sheep was, however, fairly appraised, and the Cagot paid no more for it than any other man would have done.

Did a Cagot leave his poor cabin, and venture into the towns, even to render services required of him in the way of his trade, he was bidden, by all the municipal laws, to stand by and remember his rude old state. In all the towns and villages the large districts extending on both sides of the Pyrenees—in all that part of Spain—they were forbidden to buy or sell anything eatable, to walk in the middle (esteemed the better) part of the streets, to come within the gates before sunrise, or to be found after sunset within the walls of the town. But still, as the Cagots were good-looking men, and (although they bore certain natural marks of their caste, of which I shall speak by-and-by) were not easily distinguished by casual passers-by from other men, they were compelled to wear some distinctive peculiarity which should arrest the eye; and, in the greater number of towns, it was decreed that the outward sign of a Cagot should be a piece of red cloth sewed conspicuously on the front of his dress. In other towns, the mark of Cagoterie was the foot of a duck or a goose hung over their left shoulder, so as to be seen by any one meeting them. After a time, the more convenient badge of a

66

piece of yellow cloth cut out in the shape of a duck's foot, was adopted. If any Cagot was found in any town or village without his badge, he had to pay a fine of five sous, and to lose his dress. He was expected to shrink away from any passer-by, for fear that their clothes should touch each other; or else to stand still in some corner or by-place. If the Cagots were thirsty during the days which they passed in those towns where their presence was barely suffered, they had no means of quenching their thirst, for they were forbidden to enter into the little cabarets or taverns. Even the water gushing out of the common fountain was prohibited to them. Far away, in their own squalid village, there was the Cagot fountain, and they were not allowed to drink of any other water. A Cagot woman having to make purchases in the town, was liable to be flogged out of it if she went to buy anything except on a Monday—a day on which all other people who could, kept their houses for fear of coming in contact with the accursed race.

In the Pays Basque, the prejudices—and for some time the laws—ran stronger against them than any which I have hitherto mentioned. The Basque Cagot was not allowed to possess sheep. He might keep a pig for provision, but his pig had no right of pasturage. He might cut and carry grass for the ass, which was the only other animal he was permitted to own; and this ass was permitted, because its existence was rather an advantage to the oppressor, who constantly availed himself of the Cagot's mechanical skill, and was glad to have him and his tools easily conveyed from one place to another.

The race was repulsed by the State. Under the small local governments they could hold no post whatsoever. And they were barely tolerated by the Church, although they were good Catholics, and zealous frequenters of the mass. They might only enter the churches by a small door set apart for them, through which no one of the pure race ever passed. This door was low, so as to compel them to make an obeisance. It was occasionally surrounded by sculpture, which invariably represented an oak-branch with a dove above it. When they were once in, they might not go to the holy water used by others. They had a bénitier of their own; nor were they allowed to share in the consecrated bread when that was handed round to the believers of the pure race. The Cagots stood afar off, near the door. There were certain boundaries—imaginary lines on the nave and in the aisles which they might not pass. In one or two of the more tolerant of the Pyrenean villages, the blessed bread was offered to the Cagots, the priest standing on one side of the boundary, and giving the pieces of bread on a long wooden fork to each person successively.

When the Cagot died, he was interred apart, in a plot burying-ground on the north side of the cemetery. Under such laws and prescriptions as I have described, it is no wonder that he was generally too poor to have much property for his children to inherit; but certain descriptions of it were forfeited to the commune. The only possession which all who were not of his own race refused to touch, was his furniture. That was tainted, infectious, unclean—fit for none but Cagots.

When such were, for at least three centuries, the prevalent usages and opinions with regard to this oppressed race, it is not surprising that we read of occasional outbursts of ferocious violence on their part. In the Basses-Pyrenées, for instance it is only about a hundred years since, that the Cagots of Rehouilhes rose up against the inhabitants of the neighbouring town of Lourdes, and got the better of them, by their magical powers as it is said. The people of Lourdes were conquered and slain, and their ghastly, bloody heads served the triumphant Cagots for balls to play at ninepins with! The local parliaments had begun, by this time, to perceive how oppressive was the ban of public opinion under which the Cagots lay, and were not inclined to enforce too severe a punishment. Accordingly, the decree of the parliament of Toulouse condemned only the leading Cagots concerned in this affray to be put to death, and that henceforward and for ever no Cagot was to be permitted to enter the town of Lourdes by any gate but that called Capdet-pourtet: they were only to be allowed to walk under the rain-gutters, and neither to sit, eat, nor drink in the town. If they failed in observing any of these rules, the parliament decreed, in the spirit of Shylock, that the disobedient Cagots should have two strips of flesh, weighing never more than two ounces a-piece, cut out from each side of their spines.

In the fourteenth, fifteenth, and sixteenth centuries it was considered no more a crime to kill a Cagot than to destroy obnoxious vermin. A "nest of Cagots," as the old accounts phrase it, had assembled in a deserted castle of Mauvezin, about the year sixteen hundred; and, certainly, they made themselves not very agreeable neighbours, as they seemed to enjoy their reputation of magicians; and, by some acoustic secrets which were known to them, all sorts of moanings and groanings were heard in the neighbouring forests, very much to the alarm of the good people of the pure race; who could not cut off a withered branch for firewood, but some unearthly sound seemed to fill the air, nor drink water which was not poisoned, because the Cagots would persist in filling their pitchers at the same running stream. Added to these grievances, the various pilferings perpetually going on in the neighbourhood made the inhabitants of the adjacent towns and hamlets believe that they had a very sufficient cause for wishing to murder all the Cagots in the Château de Mauvezin. But it was surrounded by a moat, and only accessible by a drawbridge; besides which, the Cagots were fierce and vigilant. Some one, however, proposed to get into their confidence; and for this purpose he pretended to fall ill close to their path, so that on returning to their stronghold they perceived him, and took him in, restored him to health, and made a friend of him. One day, when they were all playing at ninepins in the woods, their treacherous friend left the party on pretence of being thirsty, and went back into the castle, drawing up the bridge after he had passed over it, and so cutting off their means of escape into safety. Them, going up to the highest part of the castle, he blew a horn, and the pure race, who were lying in wait on the watch for some such signal, fell upon the Cagots at their games, and slew them all. For this murder I find no punishment decreed in the parliament of Toulouse, or elsewhere.

As any intermarriage with the pure race was strictly forbidden, and as there were books kept in every commune in which the names and habitations of the reputed Cagots were written, these unfortunate people had no hope of ever becoming blended with the rest of the population. Did a Cagot marriage take place, the couple were serenaded with satirical songs. They also had minstrels, and many of their romances are still current in Brittany; but they did not attempt to make any reprisals of satire or abuse. Their disposition was amiable, and their intelligence great. Indeed, it required both these qualities, and their great love of mechanical labour, to make their lives tolerable.

At last, they began to petition that they might receive some protection from the laws; and, towards the end of the seventeenth century, the judicial power took their side. But they gained little by this. Law could not prevail against custom: and, in the ten or twenty years just preceding the first French revolution, the prejudice in France against the Cagots amounted to fierce and positive abhorrence.

At the beginning of the sixteenth century, the Cagots of Navarre complained to the Pope, that they were excluded from the fellowship of men, and accursed by the Church, because their ancestors had given help to a certain Count Raymond of Toulouse in his revolt against the Holy See. They entreated his holiness not to visit upon them the sins of their fathers. The Pope issued a bull on the thirteenth of May, fifteen hundred and fifteen—ordering them to be well-treated and to be admitted to the same privileges as other men. He charged Don Juan de Santa Maria of Pampeluna to see to the execution of this bull. But Don Juan was slow to help, and the poor Spanish Cagots grew impatient, and resolved to try the secular power. They accordingly applied to the Cortes of Navarre, and were opposed on a variety of grounds. First, it was stated that their ancestors had had "nothing to do with Raymond Count of Toulouse, or with any such knightly personage; that they were in fact descendants of Gehazi, servant of Elisha (second book of Kings,

71

fifth chapter, twenty-seventh verse), who had been accursed by his master for his fraud upon Naaman, and doomed, he and his descendants, to be lepers for evermore. Name, Cagots or Gahets; Gahets, Gehazites. What can be more clear? And if that is not enough, and you tell us that the Cagots are not lepers now; we reply that there are two kinds of leprosy, one perceptible and the other imperceptible, even to the person suffering from it. Besides, it is the country talk, that where the Cagot treads, the grass withers, proving the unnatural heat of his body. Many credible and trustworthy witnesses will also tell you that, if a Cagot holds a freshly-gathered apple in his hand, it will shrivel and wither up in an hour's time as much as if it had been kept for a whole winter in a dry room. They are born with tails; although the parents are cunning enough to pinch them off immediately. Do you doubt this? If it is not true, why do the children of the pure race delight in sewing on sheep's tails to the dress of any Cagot who is so absorbed in his work as not to perceive them? And their bodily smell is so horrible and detestable that it shows that they must be heretics of some vile and pernicious description, for do we not read of the incense of good workers, and the fragrance of holiness?"

Such were literally the arguments by which the Cagots were thrown back into a worse position than ever, as far as regarded their rights as citizens. The Pope insisted that they should receive all their ecclesiastical privileges. The Spanish priests said nothing; but tacitly refused to allow the Cagots to mingle with the rest of the faithful, either dead or alive. The accursed race obtained laws in their favour from the Emperor Charles the Fifth; which, however, there was no one to carry into effect. As a sort of revenge for their want of submission, and for their impertinence in daring to complain, their tools were all taken away from them by the local authorities: an old man and all his family died of starvation, being no longer allowed to fish.

They could not emigrate. Even to remove their poor mud habitations, from one spot to another, excited anger and suspicion. To be sure, in sixteen hundred and ninety-five, the Spanish government ordered the alcaldes to search out all the Cagots, and to expel them before two months had expired, under pain of having fifty ducats to pay for every Cagot remaining in Spain at the expiration of that time. The inhabitants of the villages rose up and flogged out any of the miserable race who might be in their neighbourhood; but the French were on their guard against this enforced irruption, and refused to permit them to enter France. Numbers were hunted up into the inhospitable Pyrenees, and there died of starvation, or became a prey to wild beasts. They were obliged to wear both gloves and shoes when they were thus put to flight, otherwise the stones and herbage they trod upon and the balustrades of the bridges that they handled in crossing, would, according to popular belief, have become poisonous.

And all this time, there was nothing remarkable or disgusting in the outward appearance of this unfortunate people. There was nothing about them to countenance the idea of their being lepers—the most natural mode of accounting for the abhorrence in which they were held. They were repeatedly examined by learned doctors, whose experiments, although singular and rude, appear to have been made in a spirit of humanity. For instance, the surgeons of the king of Navarre, in sixteen hundred, bled twenty-two Cagots, in order to examine and analyze their blood. They were young and healthy people of both sexes; and the doctors seem to have expected that they should have been able to extract some new kind of salt from their blood which might account for the wonderful heat of their bodies. But their blood was just like that of other people. Some of these medical men have left us a description of the general appearance of this unfortunate race, at a time when they were more numerous and less intermixed than they are now. The families existing in the south and west of France, who are reputed to be of Cagot descent at this day, are, like their ancestors, tall, largely made, and powerful in frame; fair and ruddy in complexion, with gray-blue eyes, in which some observers see a pensive heaviness of look. Their lips are thick, but well-formed. Some of the reports name their sad expression of countenance with surprise and suspicion—"They are not gay, like other folk." The wonder would be if they were. Dr. Guyon, the medical man of the last century who has left the clearest report on the health of the Cagots, speaks of the vigorous old age they attain to. In one family alone, he found a man of seventy-four years of age; a woman as old, gathering cherries; and another woman, aged eighty-three, was lying on the grass, having her hair combed by her great-grandchildren. Dr. Guyon and other surgeons examined into the subject of the horribly infectious smell which the Cagots were said to leave behind them, and upon everything they touched; but they could perceive nothing unusual on this head. They also examined their ears, which according to common belief (a belief existing to this day), were differently shaped from those of other people; being round and gristly, without the lobe of flesh into which the ear-ring is inserted. They decided that most of the Cagots whom they examined had the ears of this round shape; but they gravely added, that they saw no reason why this should exclude them from the good-will of men, and from the power of holding office in Church and State. They recorded the fact, that the children of the towns ran baaing after any Cagot who had been compelled to come into the streets to make purchases, in allusion to this peculiarity of the shape of the ear, which bore some resemblance to the ears of the sheep as they are cut by the shepherds in this district. Dr. Guyon names the case of a beautiful Cagot girl, who sang most sweetly, and prayed to be allowed to sing canticles in the organ-loft. The organist, more musician than bigot, allowed her to come, but the indignant congregation, finding out whence proceeded that clear, fresh voice, rushed up to the organ-loft, and chased the girl out, bidding her "remember her ears," and not commit the sacrilege of singing praises to God along with the pure race.

But this medical report of Dr. Guyon's—bringing facts and arguments to confirm his opinion, that there was no physical reason why the Cagots should not be received on terms of social equality by the rest of the world—did no more for his clients than the legal decrees promulgated two centuries before had done. The French proved the truth of the saying in Hudibras—

> He that's convinced against his will
> Is of the same opinion still.

And, indeed, the being convinced by Dr. Guyon that they ought to receive Cagots as fellow-creatures, only made them more rabid in declaring that they would not. One or two little occurrences which are recorded, show that the bitterness of the repugnance to the Cagots was in full force at the time just preceding the first French revolution. There was a M. d'Abedos, the curate of Lourdes, and brother to the seigneur of the neighbouring castle, who was living in seventeen hundred and eighty; he was well-educated for the time, a travelled man, and sensible and moderate in all respects but that of his abhorrence of the Cagots: he would insult them from the very altar, calling out to them, as they stood afar off, "Oh! ye Cagots, damned for evermore!" One day, a half-blind Cagot stumbled and touched the censer borne before this Abbé de Lourdes. He was immediately turned out of the church, and forbidden ever to re-enter it. One does not know how to account for the fact, that the very brother of this bigoted abbé, the seigneur of the village, went and married a Cagot girl; but so it was, and the abbé brought a legal process against him, and had his estates taken from him, solely on account of his marriage, which reduced him to the condition of a Cagot, against whom the old law was still in force. The descendants of this Seigneur de Lourdes are simple peasants at this very day, working on the lands which belonged to their grandfather.

This prejudice against mixed marriages remained prevalent until very lately. The tradition of the Cagot descent lingered among the people, long after the laws against the accursed race were abolished. A Breton girl, within the last few years, having two lovers each of reputed Cagot descent, employed a notary to examine their pedigrees, and see which of the two had least Cagot in him; and to that one she gave her hand. In Brittany the prejudice seems to have been more virulent than anywhere else. M. Emile Souvestre records proofs of the hatred borne to them in

Brittany so recently as in eighteen hundred and thirty-five. Just lately a baker at Hennebon, having married a girl of Cagot descent, lost all his custom. The godfather and godmother of a Cagot child became Cagots themselves by the Breton laws, unless, indeed, the poor little baby died before attaining a certain number of days. They had to eat the butchers' meat condemned as unhealthy; but, for some unknown reason, they were considered to have a right to every cut loaf turned upside down, with its cut side towards the door, and might enter any house in which they saw a loaf in this position, and carry it away with them. About thirty years ago, there was the skeleton of a hand hanging up as an offering in a Breton church near Quimperle, and the tradition was, that it was the hand of a rich Cagot who had dared to take holy water out of the usual bénitier, some time at the beginning of the reign of Louis the Sixteenth; which an old soldier witnessing, he lay in wait, and the next time the offender approached the bénitier he cut off his hand, and hung it up, dripping with blood, as an offering to the patron saint of the church. The poor Cagots in Brittany petitioned against their opprobrious name, and begged to be distinguished by the appelation of Malandrins. To English ears one is much the same as the other, as neither conveys any meaning; but, to this day, the descendants of the Cagots do not like to have this name applied to them, preferring that of Malandrin.

The French Cagots tried to destroy all the records of their pariah descent, in the commotions of seventeen hundred and eighty-nine; but if writings have disappeared, the tradition yet remains, and points out such and such a family as Cagot, or Malandrin, or Oiselier, according to the old terms of abhorrence.

There are various ways in which learned men have attempted to account for the universal repugnance in which this well-made, powerful race are held. Some say that the antipathy to them took its rise in the days when leprosy was a dreadfully prevalent disease; and that the Cagots are more liable than any other men to a kind of skin disease, not precisely leprosy, but resembling it in some of its symptoms; such as dead whiteness of complexion, and swellings of the face and extremities. There was also some resemblance to the ancient Jewish custom in respect to lepers, in the habit of the people; who on meeting a Cagot called out, "Cagote? Cagote?" to which they were bound to reply, "Perlute! perlute!" Leprosy is not properly an infectious complaint, in spite of the horror in which the Cagot furniture, and the cloth woven by them, are held in some places; the disorder is hereditary, and hence (say this body of wise men, who have troubled themselves to account for the origin of Cagoterie) the reasonableness and the justice of preventing any mixed marriages, by which this terrible tendency to leprous complaints might be spread far and wide. Another authority says, that though the Cagots are fine-looking men, hard-working, and good mechanics, yet they bear in their faces, and show in their actions, reasons for the detestation in which they are held: their glance, if you meet it, is the jettatura, or evil-eye, and they are spiteful, and cruel, and deceitful above all other men. All these qualities they derive from their ancestor Gehazi, the servant of Elisha, together with their tendency to leprosy.

Again, it is said that they are descended from the Arian Goths who were permitted to live in certain places in Guienne and Languedoc, after their defeat by King Clovis, on condition that they abjured their heresy, and kept themselves separate from all other men for ever. The principal reason alleged in support of this supposition of their Gothic descent, is the specious one of derivation,—Chiens Gots, Cans Gets, Cagots, equivalent to Dogs of Goths.

Again, they were thought to be Saracens, coming from Syria. In confirmation of this idea, was the belief that all Cagots were possessed by a horrible smell. The Lombards, also, were an unfragrant race, or so reputed among the Italians: witness Pope Stephen's letter to Charlemagne, dissuading him from marrying Bertha, daughter of Didier, King of Lombardy. The Lombards boasted of Eastern descent, and were noisome. The Cagots were noisome, and therefore must be of Eastern descent. What could be clearer? In addition, there was the proof to be derived from the name Cagot, which those maintaining the opinion of their Saracen descent held to be Chiens, or Chasseurs des Gots, because the Saracens chased the Goths out of Spain. Moreover, the Saracens were originally Mahometans, and as such obliged to bathe seven times a-day: whence the badge of the duck's foot. A duck was a water-bird: Mahometans bathed in the water. Proof upon proof!

In Brittany the common idea was, they were of Jewish descent. Their unpleasant smell was again pressed into service. The Jews, it was well known, had this physical infirmity, which might be cured either by bathing in a certain fountain in Egypt—which was a long way from Brittany—or by anointing themselves with the blood of a Christian child. Blood gushed out of the body of every Cagot on Good Friday. No wonder, if they were of Jewish descent. It was the only way of accounting for so portentous a fact. Again; the Cagots were capital carpenters, which gave the Bretons every reason to believe that their ancestors were the very Jews who made the cross. When first the tide of emigration set from Brittany to America, the oppressed Cagots crowded to the ports, seeking to go to some new country, where their race might be unknown. Here was another proof of their descent from Abraham and his nomadic people: and, the forty years' wandering in the wilderness and the Wandering Jew himself, were pressed into the service to prove that the Cagots derived their restlessness and love of change from their ancestors, the Jews. The Jews, also, practised arts-magic, and the Cagots sold bags of wind to the Breton sailors, enchanted maidens to love them—maidens who never would have cared for them, unless they had been previously enchanted—made hollow rocks and trees give out strange and unearthly noises, and sold the magical herb called bon-succès. It is true enough that, in all the early acts of the fourteenth century, the same laws apply to Jews as to Cagots, and the appellations seem used indiscriminately; but their fair complexions, their remarkable devotion to all the ceremonies of the Catholic Church, and many other circumstances, conspire to forbid our believing them to be of Hebrew descent.

Another very plausible idea is, that they are the descendants of unfortunate individuals afflicted with goitres, which is, even to this day, not an uncommon disorder in the gorges and valleys of the Pyrenees. Some have even derived the word goitre from Got, or Goth; but their name, Crestia, is not unlike Cretin, and the same symptoms of idiotism were not unusual among the Cagots; although sometimes, if old tradition is to be credited, their malady of the brain took rather the form of violent delirium, which attacked them at new and full moons. Then the workmen laid down their tools, and rushed off from their labour to play mad pranks up and down the country. Perpetual motion was required to alleviate the agony of fury that seized upon the Cagots at such times. In this desire for rapid movement, the attack resembled the Neapolitan tarantella; while in the mad deeds they performed during such attacks, they were not unlike the northern Berserker. In Béarn especially, those suffering from this madness were dreaded by the pure race; the Béarnais, going to cut their wooden clogs in the great forests that lay around the base of the Pyrenées, feared above all things to go too near the periods when the Cagoutelle seized on the oppressed and accursed people; from whom it was then the oppressors' turn to fly. A man was living within the memory of some, who married a Cagot wife; he used to beat her right soundly when he saw the first symptoms of the Cagoutelle, and, having reduced her to a wholesome state of exhaustion and insensibility, he locked her up until the moon had altered her shape in the heavens. If he had not taken such decided steps, say the oldest inhabitants, there is no knowing what might have happened.

From the thirteenth to the end of the nineteenth century, there are facts enough to prove the universal abhorrence in which this unfortunate race was held; whether called Cagots, or Gahets in Pyrenean districts, Caqueaux in Brittany, or Yaqueros Asturias. The great French revolution brought some good out of its fermentation of the people: the more intelligent among them tried to overcome the prejudice against the Cagots.

In seventeen hundred and eighteen, there was a famous cause

tried at Biarritz relating to Cagot rights and privileges. There was a wealthy miller, Etienne Arnauld by name, of the race of Gotz, Quagotz, Bisigotz, Astragotz, or Gahetz, as his people are described in the legal document. He married an heiress, a Gotte (or Cagot) of Biarritz; and the newly-married well-to-do couple saw no reason why they should stand near the door in the church, nor why he should not hold some civil office in the commune, of which he was the principal inhabitant. Accordingly, he petitioned the law that he and his wife might be allowed to sit in the gallery of the church, and that he might be relieved from his civil disabilities. This wealthy white miller, Etienne Arnauld, pursued his rights with some vigour against the Baillie of Labourd, the dignitary of the neighbourhood. Whereupon the inhabitants of Biarritz met in the open air, on the eighth of May, to the number of one hundred and fifty; approved of the conduct of the Baillie in rejecting Arnauld, made a subscription, and gave all power to their lawyers to defend the cause of the pure race against Etienne Arnauld — "that stranger," who, having married a girl of Cagot blood, ought also to be expelled from the holy places. This lawsuit was carried through all the local courts, and ended by an appeal to the highest court in Paris; where a decision was given against Basque superstitions; and Etienne Arnauld was thenceforward entitled to enter the gallery of the church.

Of course, the inhabitants of Biarritz were all the more ferocious for having been conquered; and, four years later, a carpenter, named Miguel Legaret, suspected of Cagot descent, having placed himself in the church among other people, was dragged out by the abbé and two of the jurets of the parish. Legaret defended himself with a sharp knife at the time, and went to law afterwards; the end of which was, that the abbé and his two accomplices were condemned to a public confession of penitence, to be uttered while on their knees at the church door, just after high-mass. They appealed to the parliament of Bourdeaux against this decision, but met with no better success than the opponents of the miller Arnauld. Legaret was confirmed in his right of standing where he would in the parish church. That a living Cagot had equal rights with other men in the town of Biarritz seemed now ceded to them; but a dead Cagot was a different thing. The inhabitants of pure blood struggled long and hard to be interred apart from the abhorred race. The Cagots were equally persistent in claiming to have a common burying-ground. Again the texts of the Old Testament were referred to, and the pure blood quoted triumphantly the precedent of Uzziah the leper (twenty-sixth chapter of the second book of Chronicles), who was buried in the field of the Sepulchres of the Kings, not in the sepulchres themselves. The Cagots pleaded that they were healthy and able-bodied; with no taint of leprosy near them. They were met by the strong argument so difficult to be refuted, which I quoted before. Leprosy was of two kinds, perceptible and imperceptible. If the Cagots were suffering from the latter kind, who could tell whether they were free from it or not? That decision must be left to the judgment of others.

One sturdy Cagot family alone, Belone by name, kept up a lawsuit, claiming the privilege of common sepulture, for forty-two years; although the curé of Biarritz had to pay one hundred livres for every Cagot not interred in the right place. The inhabitants indemnified the curate for all these fines.

M. de Romagne, Bishop of Tarbes, who died in seventeen hundred and sixty-eight, was the first to allow a Cagot to fill any office in the Church. To be sure, some were so spiritless as to reject office when it was offered to them, because, by so claiming their equality, they had to pay the same taxes as other men, instead of the Rancale or pole-tax levied on the Cagots; the collector of which had also a right to claim a piece of bread of a certain size for his dog at every Cagot dwelling.

Even in the present century, it has been necessary in some churches for the archdeacon of the district, followed by all his clergy, to pass out of the small door previously appropriated to the Cagots, in order to mitigate the superstition which, even so lately, made the people refuse to mingle with them in the house of God. A Cagot once played the congregation at Larroque a trick suggested by what I have just named. He slily locked the great parish-door of the church, while the greater part of the inhabitants were assisting at mass inside; put gravel into the lock itself, so as to prevent the use of any duplicate key,—and had the pleasure of seeing the proud pure-blooded people file out with bended head, through the small low door used by the abhorred Cagots.

We are naturally shocked at discovering, from facts such as these, the causeless rancour with which innocent and industrious people were so recently persecuted. The moral of the history of the accursed race may, perhaps, be best conveyed

in the words of an epitaph on Mrs. Mary Hand, who lies buried
in the churchyard of Stratford-on-Avon:—

> What faults you saw in me,
>   Pray strive to shun;
> And look at home; there's
>   Something to be done.

ROUND THE SOFA

[Project Gutenberg note: Elizabeth Gaskell wrote the following story to join together a number of her other, previously published, short stories. Project Gutenberg has already released the other stories and so they are not repeated here—however, notes are given at the appropriate places.—DP.]

Long ago I was placed by my parents under the medical treatment of a certain Mr. Dawson, a surgeon in Edinburgh, who had obtained a reputation for the cure of a particular class of diseases. I was sent with my governess into lodgings near his house, in the Old Town. I was to combine lessons from the excellent Edinburgh masters, with the medicines and exercises needed for my indisposition. It was at first rather dreary to leave my brothers and sisters, and to give up our merry out-of-doors life with our country home, for dull lodgings, with only poor grave Miss Duncan for a companion; and to exchange our romps in the garden and rambles through the fields for stiff walks in the streets, the decorum of which obliged me to tie my bonnet-strings neatly, and put on my shawl with some regard to straightness.

The evenings were the worst. It was autumn, and of course they daily grew longer: they were long enough, I am sure, when we first settled down in those gray and drab lodgings. For, you must know, my father and mother were not rich, and there were a great many of us, and the medical expenses to be incurred by my being placed under Mr. Dawson's care were expected to be considerable; therefore, one great point in our search after lodgings was economy. My father, who was too true a gentleman to feel false shame, had named this necessity for cheapness to Mr. Dawson; and in return, Mr. Dawson had told him of those at No. 6 Cromer Street, in which we were finally settled. The house belonged to an old man, at one time a tutor to young men preparing for the University, in which capacity he had become known to Mr. Dawson. But his pupils had dropped off; and when we went to lodge with him, I imagine that his principal support was derived from a few occasional lessons which he gave, and from letting the rooms that we took, a drawing-room opening into a bed-room, out of which a smaller chamber led. His daughter was his housekeeper: a son, whom we never saw, supposed to be leading the same life that his father had done before him, only we never saw or heard of any pupils; and there was one hard-working, honest little Scottish maiden, square, stumpy, neat, and plain, who might have been any age from eighteen to forty.

Looking back on the household now, there was perhaps much to admire in their quiet endurance of decent poverty; but at this time, their poverty grated against many of my tastes, for I could not recognize the fact, that in a town the simple graces of fresh flowers, clean white muslin curtains, pretty bright chintzes, all cost money, which is saved by the adoption of dust-coloured moreen, and mud-coloured carpets. There was not a penny spent on mere elegance in that room; yet there was everything considered necessary to comfort: but after all, such mere pretences of comfort! a hard, slippery, black horse-hair sofa,

87

which was no place of rest; an old piano, serving as a sideboard; a grate, narrowed by an inner supplement, till it hardly held a handful of the small coal which could scarcely ever be stirred up into a genial blaze. But there were two evils worse than even this coldness and bareness of the rooms: one was that we were provided with a latch-key, which allowed us to open the front door whenever we came home from a walk, and go upstairs without meeting any face of welcome, or hearing the sound of a human voice in the apparently deserted house—Mr. Mackenzie piqued himself on the noiselessness of his establishment; and the other, which might almost seem to neutralize the first, was the danger we were always exposed to on going out, of the old man—sly, miserly, and intelligent—popping out upon us from his room, close to the left hand of the door, with some civility which we learned to distrust as a mere pretext for extorting more money, yet which it was difficult to refuse: such as the offer of any books out of his library, a great temptation, for we could see into the shelf-lined room; but just as we were on the point of yielding, there was a hint of the "consideration" to be expected for the loan of books of so much higher a class than any to be obtained at the circulating library, which made us suddenly draw back. Another time he came out of his den to offer us written cards, to distribute among our acquaintance, on which he undertook to teach the very things I was to learn; but I would rather have been the most ignorant woman that ever lived than tried to learn anything from that old fox in breeches. When we had declined all his proposals, he went apparently into dudgeon. Once when we had forgotten our latch-key we rang in vain for many times at the door, seeing our landlord standing all the time at the window to the right, looking out of it in an absent and philosophical state of mind, from which no signs and gestures of ours could arouse him.

The women of the household were far better, and more really respectable, though even on them poverty had laid her heavy left hand, instead of her blessing right. Miss Mackenzie kept us as short in our food as she decently could—we paid so much a week for our board, be it observed; and if one day we had less appetite than another our meals were docked to the smaller standard, until Miss Duncan ventured to remonstrate. The sturdy maid-of-all-work was scrupulously honest, but looked discontented, and scarcely vouchsafed us thanks, when on leaving we gave her what Mrs. Dawson had told us would be considered handsome in most lodgings. I do not believe Phenice ever received wages from the Mackenzies.

But that dear Mrs. Dawson! The mention of her comes into my mind like the bright sunshine into our dingy little drawing room came on those days;—as a sweet scent of violets greets the sorrowful passer among the woodlands.

Mrs. Dawson was not Mr. Dawson's wife, for he was a bachelor. She was his crippled sister, an old maid, who had, what she called, taken her brevet rank.

After we had been about a fortnight in Edinburgh, Mr. Dawson said, in a sort of half doubtful manner to Miss Duncan—

"My sister bids me say, that every Monday evening a few friends come in to sit round her sofa for an hour or so,—some before going to gayer parties—and that if you and Miss Greatorex would like a little change, she would only be too glad to see you. Any time from seven to eight to-night; and I must add my injunctions, both for her sake, and for that of my little patient's, here, that you leave at nine o'clock. After all, I do not know if you will care to come; but Margaret bade me ask you;" and he glanced up suspiciously and sharply at us. If either of us had felt the slightest reluctance, however well disguised by manner, to accept this invitation, I am sure he would have at once detected our feelings, and withdrawn it; so jealous and chary was he of anything pertaining to the appreciation of this beloved sister.

But if it had been to spend an evening at the dentist's, I believe I should have welcomed the invitation, so weary was I of the monotony of the nights in our lodgings; and as for Miss Duncan, an invitation to tea was of itself a pure and unmixed honour, and one to be accepted with all becoming form and gratitude: so Mr. Dawson's sharp glances over his spectacles failed to detect anything but the truest pleasure, and he went on.

"You'll find it very dull, I dare say. Only a few old fogies like myself, and one or two good sweet young women: I never know who'll come. Margaret is obliged to lie in a darkened room— only half-lighted I mean,—because her eyes are weak,—oh, it will be very stupid, I dare say: don't thank me till you've been once and tried it, and then if you like it, your best thanks will be to come again every Monday, from half-past seven to nine, you know. Good-bye, good-bye."

Hitherto I had never been out to a party of grown-up people; and no court ball to a London young lady could seem more redolent of honour and pleasure than this Monday evening to me.

Dressed out in new stiff book-muslin, made up to my throat,—a frock which had seemed to me and my sisters the height of earthly grandeur and finery—Alice, our old nurse, had been making it at home, in contemplation of the possibility of such an event during my stay in Edinburgh, but which had then appeared to me a robe too lovely and angelic to be ever worn short of heaven—I went with Miss Duncan to Mr. Dawson's at the appointed time. We entered through one small lofty room, perhaps I ought to call it an antechamber, for the house was old-fashioned, and stately and grand, the large square drawing-room, into the centre of which Mrs. Dawson's sofa was drawn. Behind her a little was placed a table with a great cluster candlestick upon it, bearing seven or eight wax-lights; and that was all the light in the room, which looked to me very vast and indistinct after our pinched-up apartment at the Mackenzie's. Mrs. Dawson must have been sixty; and yet her face looked very soft and smooth and child-like. Her hair was quite gray: it would have looked white but for the snowiness of her cap, and satin ribbon. She was wrapped in a kind of dressing-gown of French grey merino: the furniture of the room was deep rose-colour, and white and gold,—the paper which covered the walls was Indian, beginning low down with a profusion of tropical leaves and birds and insects, and gradually diminishing in richness of detail till at the top it ended in the most delicate tendrils and most filmy insects.

Mr. Dawson had acquired much riches in his profession, and his house gave one this impression. In the corners of the rooms were great jars of Eastern china, filled with flower-leaves and spices; and in the middle of all this was placed the sofa, which poor Margaret Dawson passed whole days, and months, and years, without the power of moving by herself. By-and-by Mrs. Dawson's maid brought in tea and macaroons for us, and a little cup of milk and water and a biscuit for her. Then the door opened. We had come very early, and in came Edinburgh professors, Edinburgh beauties, and celebrities, all on their way to some other gayer and later party, but coming first to see Mrs. Dawson, and tell her their bon-mots, or their interests, or their plans. By each learned man, by each lovely girl, she was treated as a dear friend, who knew something more about their own individual selves, independent of their reputation and general society-character, than any one else.

It was very brilliant and very dazzling, and gave enough to think about and wonder about for many days.

Monday after Monday we went, stationary, silent; what could we find to say to any one but Mrs. Margaret herself? Winter passed, summer was coming, still I was ailing, and weary of my life; but still Mr. Dawson gave hopes of my ultimate recovery. My father and mother came and went; but they could not stay long, they had so many claims upon them. Mrs. Margaret Dawson had become my dear friend, although, perhaps, I had never exchanged as many words with her as I had with Miss Mackenzie, but then with Mrs. Dawson every word was a pearl or a diamond.

People began to drop off from Edinburgh, only a few were left, and I am not sure if our Monday evenings were not all the pleasanter.

There was Mr. Sperano, the Italian exile, banished even from

France, where he had long resided, and now teaching Italian with meek diligence in the northern city; there was Mr. Preston, the Westmoreland squire, or, as he preferred to be called, statesman, whose wife had come to Edinburgh for the education of their numerous family, and who, whenever her husband had come over on one of his occasional visits, was only too glad to accompany him to Mrs. Dawson's Monday evenings, he and the invalid lady having been friends from long ago. These and ourselves kept steady visitors, and enjoyed ourselves all the more from having the more of Mrs. Dawson's society.

One evening I had brought the little stool close to her sofa, and was caressing her thin white hand, when the thought came into my head and out I spoke it.

"Tell me, dear Mrs. Dawson," said I, "how long you have been in Edinburgh; you do not speak Scotch, and Mr. Dawson says he is not Scotch."

"No, I am Lancashire—Liverpool-born," said she, smiling. "Don't you hear it in my broad tongue?"

"I hear something different to other people, but I like it because it is just you; is that Lancashire?"

"I dare say it is; for, though I am sure Lady Ludlow took pains enough to correct me in my younger days, I never could get rightly over the accent."

"Lady Ludlow," said I, "what had she to do with you? I heard you talking about her to Lady Madeline Stuart the first evening I ever came here; you and she seemed so fond of Lady Ludlow; who is she?"

"She is dead, my child; dead long ago."

I felt sorry I had spoken about her, Mrs. Dawson looked so grave and sad. I suppose she perceived my sorrow, for she went on and said—"My dear, I like to talk and to think of Lady Ludlow: she was my true, kind friend and benefactress for many years; ask me what you like about her, and do not think you give me pain."

I grew bold at this.

"Will you tell me all about her, then, please, Mrs. Dawson?"

"Nay," said she, smiling, "that would be too long a story. Here are Signor Sperano, and Miss Duncan, and Mr. and Mrs. Preston are coming to-night, Mr. Preston told me; how would they like to hear an old-world story which, after all, would be no story at all, neither beginning, nor middle, nor end, only a bundle of recollections?"

"If you speak of me, madame," said Signor Sperano, "I can only say you do me one great honour by recounting in my presence anything about any person that has ever interested you."

Miss Duncan tried to say something of the same kind. In the middle of her confused speech, Mr. and Mrs. Preston came in. I sprang up; I went to meet them.

"Oh," said I, "Mrs. Dawson is just going to tell us all about Lady Ludlow, and a great deal more, only she is afraid it won't interest anybody: do say you would like to hear it!"

Mrs. Dawson smiled at me, and in reply to their urgency she

promised to tell us all about Lady Ludlow, on condition that each one of us should, after she had ended, narrate something interesting, which we had either heard, or which had fallen within our own experience. We all promised willingly, and then gathered round her sofa to hear what she could tell us about my Lady Ludlow.

[At this point comes "My Lady Ludlow"]

As any one may guess, it had taken Mrs. Dawson several Monday evenings to narrate all this history of the days of her youth. Miss Duncan thought it would be a good exercise for me, both in memory and composition, to write out on Tuesday mornings all that I had heard the night before; and thus it came to pass that I have the manuscript of "My Lady Ludlow" now lying by me.

* * * * *

Mr. Dawson had often come in and out of the room during the time that his sister had been telling us about Lady Ludlow. He would stop, and listen a little, and smile or sigh as the case might be. The Monday after the dear old lady had wound up her tale (if tale it could be called), we felt rather at a loss what to talk about, we had grown so accustomed to listen to Mrs. Dawson. I remember I was saying, "Oh, dear! I wish some one would tell us another story!" when her brother said, as if in answer to my speech, that he had drawn up a paper all ready for the Philosophical Society, and that perhaps we might care to hear it before it was sent off: it was in a great measure compiled from a French book, published by one of the Academies, and rather dry in itself; but to which Mr. Dawson's attention had been directed, after a tour he had made in England during the past year, in which he had noticed small walled-up doors in unusual parts of some old parish churches, and had been told that they had formerly been appropriated to the use of some half-heathen race, who, before the days of gipsies, held the same outcast pariah position in most of the countries of western Europe. Mr. Dawson had been recommended to the French book which he named, as containing the fullest and most authentic account of this mysterious race, the Cagots. I did not think I should like hearing this paper as much as a story; but, of course, as he meant it kindly, we were bound to submit, and I found it, on the whole, more interesting than I anticipated.

[At this point comes "An Accursed Race"]

For some time past I had observed that Miss Duncan made a good deal of occupation for herself in writing, but that she did not like me to notice her employment. Of course this made me all the more curious; and many were my silent conjectures— some of them so near the truth that I was not much surprised when, after Mr. Dawson had finished reading his Paper to us, she hesitated, coughed, and abruptly introduced a little formal

96

speech, to the effect that she had noted down an old Welsh story the particulars of which had often been told her in her youth, as she lived close to the place where the events occurred. Everybody pressed her to read the manuscript, which she now produced from her reticule; but, when on the point of beginning, her nervousness seemed to overcome her, and she made so many apologies for its being the first and only attempt she had ever made at that kind of composition, that I began to wonder if we should ever arrive at the story at all. At length, in a high-pitched, ill-assured voice, she read out the title:

"The Doom of the Griffiths."

[At this point comes "The Doom of the Griffiths"]

You cannot think how kindly Mrs. Dawson thanked Miss Duncan for writing and reading this story. She shook my poor, pale governess so tenderly by the hand that the tears came into her eyes, and the colour to her checks.

"I though you had been so kind; I liked hearing about Lady Ludlow; I fancied, perhaps, I could do something to give a little pleasure," were the half-finished sentences Miss Duncan stammered out. I am sure it was the wish to earn similar kind words from Mrs. Dawson, that made Mrs. Preston try and rummage through her memory to see if she could not recollect some fact, or event, or history, which might interested Mrs. Dawson and the little party that gathered round her sofa. Mrs. Preston it was who told us the following tale:

97

[At this point comes "Half a Life-Time Ago"]

When this narrative was finished, Mrs. Dawson called on our two gentlemen, Signor Sperano and Mr. Preston, and told them that they had hitherto been amused or interested, but that it was now their turn to amuse or interest. They looked at each other as if this application of hers took them by surprise, and seemed altogether as much abashed as well-grown men can ever be. Signor Sperano was the first to recover himself: after thinking a little, he said—

"Your will, dear lady, is law. Next Monday evening, I will bring you an old, old story, which I found among the papers of the good old priest who first welcomed me to England. It was but a poor return for his generous kindness; but I had the opportunity of nursing him through the cholera, of which he died. He left me all that he had—no money—but his scanty furniture, his book of prayers, his crucifix and rosary, and his papers. How some of those papers came into his hands I know not. They had evidently been written many years before the venerable man was born; and I doubt whether he had ever examined the bundles, which had come down to him from some old ancestor, or in some strange bequest. His life was too busy to leave any time for the gratification of mere curiosity; I, alas! have only had too much leisure."

Next Monday, Signor Sperano read to us the story which I will call

"The Poor Clare."

[At this point comes "The Poor Clare"]

Now, of all our party who had first listened to my Lady Ludlow, Mr. Preston was the only one who had not told us something, either of information, tradition, history, or legend. We naturally turned to him; but we did not like asking him directly for his contribution, for he was a grave, reserved, and silent man.

He understood us, however, and, rousing himself as it were, he said—

"I know you wish me to tell you, in my turn, of something which I have learnt during my life. I could tell you something of my own life, and of a life dearer still to my memory; but I have shunk from narrating anything so purely personal. Yet, shrink as I will, no other but those sad recollections will present themselves to my mind. I call them sad when I think of the end of it all. However, I am not going to moralize. If my dear brother's life and death does not speak for itself, no words of mine will teach you what may be learnt from it."

[At this point comes the final story "The Half-Brothers"]

www.ingramcontent.com/pod-product-compliance
Lightning Source LLC
Chambersburg PA
CBHW011440170626
46807CB00008B/3253